I0762302

THE KING OF ACTION FIGURES

THE KING OF ACTION FIGURES

Andrew J Brandt

Caprock Publishing Group

ADVANCED PRAISE FOR

THE KING OF ACTION FIGURES

"In his newest novel, Andrew J Brandt masterfully takes you along on a quest for the rarest of treasures. This ode to Star Wars will fill you with nostalgia and have you turning each page faster, as you join the race to hold The King of Action Figures."

- RUSSELL CAMP, AUTHOR OF *THE ANGEL OF THUNDER ROCK*

"Incredible imagination, superb storytelling skills, and the ability to hook a reader so thoroughly... Andrew J Brandt does all of this so well."

- LINDSEY JESIONOWSKI, AUTHOR OF *SHUT UP AND DANCE*

"*The King of Action Figures* shows how the fandoms we love and the friendships we form not only provide a safe space and a sense of community but can also give us the courage to believe in ourselves and our dreams."

- ALISHA EMRICH, AUTHOR OF *NERDCRUSH*

This collection is a work of fiction. Any references to historical events, real people, or real places are used fictitiously. Other names, characters, places and events are products of the author's imagination, and any resemblance to actual events or places or persons, living or dead, is entirely coincidental.

Caprock Publishing Group | 2207 S. Western, 90 | Amarillo, TX 79109

First Paperback Edition April 2024

For information about bulk, educational and other special discounts, please contact Caprock Publishing Group.

CPG can bring Andrew J Brandt to your live event. For more information or to book an event, contact Caprock Publishing Group. www.caprockpublishinggroup.com

Cover Design: Brand T Designs
Interior Design: Caprock Publishing
Editing: Brandon Biggers
ISBN: 978-1-7373487-5-7

CAPROCK PUBLISHING GROUP
AMARILLO | FT WORTH

For Ellie, whose imagination
wows me every single day.

And for Jennifer, who chose
to spend her life with a nerd.

AUTHOR'S NOTE

The rocket-firing Boba Fett action figure referenced in this novel is real. Though never released to the public (Kenner, the company that produced *Star Wars* toys through the 90's, determined that the spring-fired rocket mechanism posed a choking hazard to children) there were a few prototypes developed, including only one in full retail packaging. That figure was shown off at the New York Toy Fair in 1979. It was recently featured in an episode of The History Channel's hit TV show *Pawn Stars*.

In 2019, a prototype rocket-firing Boba Fett figure sold at auction for $185,850.

Today it is valued between $200,000 and $500,000.

-AJB
Sep 2023

else I could find. My wardrobe consisted entirely of Luke Skywalker shirts.

My drawings, too, went from simple doodles to more ornate designs and then to images that told a story. Using comic books as my template, I created panels that told my own stories about those characters, pulling ideas from my imagination and putting them down in pencil. Not too long after that, I started imagining my own stories, with my own characters.

I became an artist because my depressed, newly-single mother took me to see *Star Wars*.

If this universe really came into existence thirteen billion years ago, I could have existed at any time in history. I could have lived during the American Revolution. The Black Plague. The Renaissance.

But no.

I got to live during the time of Star Wars. When I thought everything in life was terrible, I found my meaning because of those movies.

Beyond that though, it was because of Star Wars that I got to spend two thousand miles and three days driving across the country with Katie Nguyen.

That is a miracle.

CHAPTER 1

We stood outside the exit doors of the theater, a line of Darth Vaders, Luke Skywalkers, Stormtroopers and other characters filing out around us. I had, after seeing promotional images from the movie, started to grow my hair out like Anakin Skywalker's, both of us having the same sandy brown color.

My friends and I had stood in line since noon to see this movie for its midnight release. It was called *Revenge of the Sith.* And even after fourteen hours of waiting and then watching the movie, we were high on excitement, even if it was bittersweet. We didn't want to believe that that was the last Star Wars movie, the final prequel.

The four of us had been friends since middle school, joining together in a shared sense of community. It amazes me how when you find something that you find your identity in that you attract like-minded people. Mine was a tribe of nerds who argued and came together over Star Wars, comic books and Dungeons & Dragons.

Well, three of us that is. Joel and Dustin and I met in the sixth grade. Hannah came later—she was in our freshman art class—and now Joel and she were attached at the hip. He was the lucky one of us to attain the unattainable, to find the Princess Leia to his Han Solo—a girlfriend.

Still, we welcomed her into our tribe of nerds and she fit right in, sitting at the table with us while running through a new D&D campaign or arguing over who *really* shot first (yes, I know I saw the Special Editions before the original, un-edited movies, but the answer was, and always will be, Han Solo. There is no other option).

"I can't believe that's it. That's the last *Star Wars* movie," I said. My eyes were still wide, the images in my mind fresh and I refused to let go of them.

"I know. That was the greatest thing I have ever seen in my life," Dustin said, his eyes bloodshot and bleary, his body pumped full of caffeine and theater popcorn. He had a shock of blonde hair that was almost white, and he'd been growing it out during this last year so that it now hung over his ears. It looked like a dirty mop. "I didn't want it to end."

"You know that's not going to be the last one, right?" Joel said. He was taller than the rest of us, and had been since middle school when he grew six inches the summer between sixth and seventh grades. Every single coach from then on wanted him on their teams, whether it was basketball, baseball or even football, until they saw that he ran with the gait of a newborn giraffe. By the time we were in high school, coaches looked at him the same way they looked at the rest of us, like we were second-rate citizens. Which, really, was just the way the rest of the high school elite looked at us.

"What are you talking about?" Dustin said. "That's it. That completes the saga."

Joel shook his head, his curly hair bouncing. He'd always had this head of curly hair that grew every way it damn well pleased. When we were sophomores, he buzzed it off but it just grew back even more chaotic. These days he just let it go, and it defied the laws of gravity. "You're nuts if you think that's it," he said. "Give it another ten years or so and there will be a seventh one. There's too much money to be made."

"That's ridiculous," Dustin argued. "What are they going to do? Bring the Emperor back? No way."

"I'm going again tomorrow," Hannah said to me as we listened to Joel and Dustin bicker. Sure, there were four of us, but Dustin and Joel were the heartbeat of the friend group. I didn't mind taking a backseat. And Hannah, of course, was Joel's girlfriend, which may have been an equal relationship to Joel but wholly separate from the friendship he had with Dustin. Hannah even joked sometimes that she had two boyfriends. "Eleven AM showing."

Joel turned as he heard her, a confused look on his face, and she nudged him with her hip.

"I got you a ticket too, don't worry." Hannah turned to me. "What about you, Josh? You coming with?"

"Eleven? That's in like, seven hours," I said. Even

though it was three in the morning, I didn't think I'd be going to sleep anytime soon anyway.

"I'm going to sleep, wake up and experience it all over again," Hannah said. "I have to see that lightsaber battle as many times as possible."

"Which *one*?" Dustin asked. He mimicked igniting a lightsaber and slashed it around in the air. Joel met him with his own imaginary blade and they battled in the parking lot.

Hannah and I watched this charade that almost looked choreographed. "I love that dork," she said.

"I know."

"We're going to miss you when you leave in August," she said.

I had been accepted to the Indianapolis School of Art, making my dream of becoming a comic book artist for Marvel one step closer to being a reality. That was only one step though, and I didn't know how I would be able to take the next one, or the one after that.

"We've got plenty of time to hang out before then," I said. "Plus I need Joel to finish our D&D campaign. I can't leave with the story unfinished."

"You could always adapt it into one of your comic books," she said. "He would love that."

"You know, that's not a bad idea." I had been working on my current comic book for over a year. It was a project for my acceptance into the Art Institute.

"So? You going to join us tomorrow morning?" she asked.

"No," I sighed. As much as I wanted to, I had other responsibilities. "I have to work."

The ice cream shop I worked at opened at ten in the morning and I was expected to open, which meant that I had to be there an hour before—in a little more than five hours. I would be running on fumes, but luckily not too many people were jonesing for ice cream before lunchtime. "But as soon as I'm done, you know I'm back in line for the next available showing."

"Call Joel. We'll come with you," she said. "I think he's off tomorrow."

"You're willing to see it three times in less than twenty-four hours?"

The next thing Hannah said, I understood completely.

"For Star Wars?" she said. "Anything."

CHAPTER 2

The three weeks after the release of *Revenge of the Sith* were a whirlwind. I saw the movie a total of five times. Dustin saw it eight times. I lost count for Joel and Hannah. They seemed to go to the theatre every night.

Graduation weekend also came and went, without the fanfare I expected. I mean, there were the pictures and the rehearsal and the all-night lock-in dubbed *Project Celebration* where a majority of now-graduated seniors played games until dawn. But it seemed just an item on a checklist than a cause for celebration. Just one more step on my way out of Greenwood and off to art school.

It was also sort of bittersweet. I wished my dad would have been there. It was the first time in almost nine years that I really, truly felt that I was missing out on something. I mean, I wasn't the only graduate that lived in a single-parent household, but every time I saw someone hug their own dad or take family pictures, it just made me yearn for something that I would never have again. My mom did great though, and she only cried a little, hiding her sorrow by trying her best—though, let's be honest, failing—to convince me they were happy tears.

After graduation, life sort of settled into a rhythm. I worked every day, donning the purple apron and matching cap that was the customary uniform for employees of Kaleidoscoops. It was my first job, working there since I was sixteen, slinging ice cream sundaes and milkshakes for money. While my friends had much cooler jobs—Dustin worked at the comic book store just a few blocks away from the ice cream shop while Joel worked for his dad at their family's pizza joint—the pay was pretty good and I was guaranteed every Sunday off. Still it didn't keep me from wishing that I had Dustin's luck and landed a job at the comic store instead.

When I wasn't working, the four of us were usually hanging out at Joel's house, playing video games or Dungeons & Dragons. He lived in the garage-attached apartment behind his parents, which made it our default hangout place.

Despite graduating high school, nothing really changed which, to be honest, seemed kind of sad. It was our last summer before college, the last summer of adolescence, and we were spending it huddled around a folding table, the surface littered with empty soda cans and D&D rule books as we moved miniature figures around and rolled dice.

And in the spirit of being fully transparent, part of that was me avoiding the real issue—though I'd been accepted to the Indianapolis Institute of Art, I had yet figured out how I would pay for it. There were grants and a few student loans, sure, but they didn't make up the difference in private school tuition.

On the last Saturday of June, I went into the kitchen early to find some breakfast before leaving for work. Our kitchen was built like a long hallway with appliances lining the walls. At one end sat a breakfast nook beside a large window that looked out to the front yard. Though we had a formal dining room, it was rarely used. Instead it was at the round table in the breakfast nook where we ate most of our meals. Well, we *did*. I was rarely at home for dinner these days.

As I pulled a mug from the cabinet above the coffee maker, my mom sat at the breakfast nook table, reading glasses perched at the end of her nose. Her laptop, a white Apple iBook, was opened in front of her. This was a normal Saturday for her and it amazed me how this scene changed over the years, but stayed the same. Before, it was my dad who would sit at the table on Saturday mornings, the floppy pages of a newspaper in his hands. That was a long time ago.

With my cup of coffee, I made a bowl of cereal, bringing the box of Cocoa Puffs to the table with me.

"Good morning," she said.

I mumbled a reply. I had been at Joel's house the night before and got home late.

There was a pile of mail on the counter and she

nodded to it. "There's a few for you there from that art school," she said.

I grunted a *thank you* and grabbed the envelopes, setting them on the table. I sat down in the vacant seat beside my mom and, with a mouth full of cereal, I began flipping through them. Mostly junk mail, but there were two with the logo from the school.

Of course I had high hopes that one of my many scholarship applications had been accepted and that I was now the recipient of thousands of dollars, making up the difference in what I owed in tuition. And to be honest with you, working at an ice cream shop for seven dollars an hour wasn't cutting it. I needed some of these scholarships to come through or...

There was a sound behind me, my back facing the kitchen, but I already knew who it was. Before I could even react, I had a hairy forearm around my neck.

"What's up, Banana Split?"

My brother Jake, two years older than me and still living at home, was always messing with me, trying to wrestle around like we were in middle school and not now adults. It didn't help that, even as kids, he was always twice my size.

With one arm wrapped around my neck in a half-assed chokehold, he grabbed the letter from my hands with the other, reading it.

"How embarrassing," he said. "It's not even a real school and they still don't want you."

"Jake," my mom said lazily, her eyes never coming up

from the laptop. "Leave your brother alone. He's got to go to work."

"What's it like having an art school reject you? Guess you're not as great as you think you are," Jake pestered, ignoring my mom's request. He finally did let go, plopping down in the last vacant seat at the table. He grabbed at the open box of cereal, poured a handful of chocolate spheres in his hand and munched loudly, smacking his lips.

Classic, obnoxious Jake.

We were completely different, which always confounded me. How can two bothers, from the same parents, growing up in the same house, be completely different? Two brothers who went through the same traumatic event, responded to it differently. Not just that, but even the biology of it all. He got all the athletic ability. I got the artistic gene.

One of those was much better for attracting girls in high school, and I'll let you guess which one that was.

"I've already told you," I said, repeating myself for the millionth time. "I got accepted. They didn't *reject* me."

"Bubba always says we need more hands at the shop. You can come work with me," he said, though his tone hardly cordial. Jake had reminded me, more than once, that I would *never make it in a job that takes a real man.* "Right mom? Wouldn't you prefer two sons who worked hard and made their way in the world?"

"Jake," she said, her tone now terse. "I told you that's enough."

"You wouldn't know how to make your own way if the

path was right in front of you," I spat. He was, after all, twenty years old and still living at home with mom.

"Josh" my mom said, "don't antagonize your brother."

"He started it," I argued.

"Come on, mom," Jake said, munching on more Cocoa Puffs. "I'm offering him a real job. I mean, he can't seriously think he can draw comic books forever. And scooping ice cream only pays so much."

"And you can't live here forever, yet here you are. Mom doesn't even charge you rent. At least I have a plan to move out," I said.

Jake glared at me, and I knew that I'd hit a low-blow, but I didn't really care.

"I told you," he said, his brows nearly touching from his glaring so hard, "I'm saving up to buy my own place."

"Sure you are," I said. "How much of your down payment did you spend on that Alpine sound system again? Pretty sure the speakers are worth more than your car."

He stood up, the chair squeaking hard against the linoleum floor. He made a gesture as if to hit me, his fist high.

Our mom didn't do anything but look up over her glasses, glaring at him in that way that told him that she was getting impatient already. That was all she had to do though. Jake grabbed the box of cereal and left the room.

I looked at the clock on the wall and finished my own breakfast quickly, slurping up the rest of the milk left over in my bowl.

"I'm going to work," I said, taking my dishes to the sink.

My mom mumbled an *okay*. I knew Saturday mornings were busy for her these days as she had to work doubly hard to pay all the bills and prepare for open houses during the weekend.

"I'm going to hang out with my friends afterward so I probably won't be home til late."

"And I will be going to your aunt Cathy's house this evening," she said. "So I won't be home either to make dinner."

My mom and her sister, Aunt Cathy, were both real estate agents. It was the last Saturday of the month, which meant my mom would probably be at the office all day and well into the evening. The last weekend of the month was always busiest for her, as she scheduled the properties she and Aunt Cathy would be showing for open houses throughout the next month.

"Alright. Well, I guess I'll see you guys later."

"Oh, and Josh?" she said.

I turned back to my mom as I stood in the doorway.

"Maybe a contingency plan wouldn't be such a bad idea. You could always stay at Greenwood Community College. And there's nothing wrong with living at home while you're getting an education," she said.

I sighed, almost in defeat. "Thanks," I said. "But Greenwood doesn't offer what I want." I meant the school, but I felt that way about the town as a whole as well.

I walked outside to my car, a white Jeep Cherokee

parked on the curb behind my brother's purple Mustang. The weather already warm and muggy, which meant that the shop would be full today, ice cream practically flying out the door. Days like this went by quickly and left me little time to think, which today might be a good thing. Because the only thing on my mind was how to get out of this small town and find a way to make up for the denied scholarships.

The only thing standing between me and the Indianapolis Institute of Art was money.

And the only problem was that I had just two months to figure out how to find a lot of it — twenty thousand dollars to be exact.

CHAPTER 3

I pulled up to Galaxy Comics, shedding my apron, dirty and stained with sprinkles and melted ice cream. I had been right, it was a busy shift and I was so glad to clock out six hours later. It was early afternoon and there were plenty of people walking up and down Main Street, going into and out of different shops, some enjoying a late lunch—or an early cocktail—while others were just strolling along the sidewalks. It was picturesque, the way you would imagine your hometown would look when you're reminiscing on the *good ol' days*.

Galaxy Comics was sort of tucked away on the main strip, secluded from the higher-end stores that sold things like boots and wedding dresses. The sign that hung on the building's overhang, the words *Galaxy Comics* overlayed on a spiral galaxy, was a simple painted piece of vinyl, much different from the lit-up signs on top of the other businesses. It was easy to miss, easy to ignore, which I think is how Edward Reynolds, the guy that ran the joint, liked it. He was a peculiar man, and I'd only met him only a handful of times. Dustin said he only came in to check inventory and do payroll or if a special guest came through town—a no-name comic book artist or a has-been C-level actor on their way to a comic convention in Indianapolis perhaps—but other than that, the shop was mostly ran by Dustin and a handful of other nerds and Greenwood social outcasts.

I walked inside Galaxy, the brass bell above the door ringing above me.

"Welcome to Galaxy—" Dustin started, almost out of habit until he looked up through the mop of blonde hair that fell in front of his eyes. He hopped off the chair behind the checkout counter. "Oh! Dude! How's it going?"

"Hey man," I said, walking up to him, glancing at the new release comics and memorabilia on the shelves. The store was set up in two main areas. The retail area was up front with the comic books, Dungeons and Dragons game books, Magic: the Gathering cards, stuff like that in a small display room, and then a larger open room to the side where people could sit at one of the tables arranged in there and play a game of Warhammer or D&D. It was a fun hangout place in a town where those were few and far between. And, for guys like me and my friends, it was the only place to go other than Joel's house.

The shop was relatively busy for a Saturday afternoon. There were a few people playing table top games in the gaming space. There were some customers thumbing through a box of old comic book back issues. The new releases were out on display on wire racks, but the back issues were stored in long cardboard boxes on the tables, in alphabetical order by publisher.

"How's things at Kaleidoscoops?" he asked, putting away the comic book he'd been reading.

The atmosphere in here was much different from the ice cream shop. My every move was watched by not only the people whose sundae I was concocting, but also my boss, Mr. Gilroy. He was a micromanager of the highest order, making my working life a living hell. I could never have enough time to just sit and read a comic book while other people perused or played games. I couldn't imagine how much drawing I would get done if I could work in a place like Galaxy Comics. I'd probably have my own comic book done by now.

"Same as always," I said with a shrug.

"That bad, huh?"

"Yeah," I said. "Mr. Gilroy literally weighed the hot fudge container after every sundae, saying I was putting on too much on the ice cream and eating all the profit."

"If I worked there, I literally *would* eat all the profits," he said. "I'd keep a spoon in my pocket. I would be so fat dude."

"And," I said, cutting him off, "the health inspector would shut you down immediately."

Dustin laughed. "Luckily there's no health inspector at a comic book shop."

"Well, we also don't charge table fees to hang out," I

said, eyeing a sign at the front desk that read the new fees for sitting to play a game.

"Hey, it's not my fault," he said, his hands up. "Mr. Reynolds said we weren't charging enough."

I shook my head. Table fees, I thought, were a greedy way to extract more money from a customer base. They were essentially a charge to use the space to play games—usually games or cards that you had already purchased from the shop.

"Oh, hey, check this out," Dustin said, hopping from his barstool and coming out from behind the checkout counter.

He gestured for me to follow him to the other side of the retail area, towards a glass display case where they held some of the most valuable items in the store. I don't know how many times I'd salivated over some of the contents that had lived in that case over the years. There were autographed copies of *The Walking Dead*, a few figurines and even a prop lightsaber that was actually used in the filming of *Return of the Jedi*.

"We got this in yesterday," he said, unlocking the cabinet.

He pulled out a framed photograph, a still image of the lightsaber battle between Anakin Skywalker and Obi-Wan Kenobi, the climax of the new film. It was autographed by both actors with a certificate of authenticity.

"Wow," I said as Dustin handed me the photo.

"Yeah. Darth freaking Vader touched that. And now you have too."

"Where did you guys even get that?"

"Mr. Reynolds scours the internet for collectibles through estate sales," he said. "Most newspapers these days put their stuff online so he is constantly looking for things he can buy cheap and sell here."

"That's not a bad idea." The only thing I ever used the internet for was searching for bootleg Dragonball videos from Japan or downloading music through file sharing websites. Seeing this made me wonder what I could find to add to my collection of memorabilia at home.

"And then we get to stare at it all day," Dustin said, almost wistfully. I knew how he felt.

"Why can't I work here again?" I asked, almost whining. A comic book shop would be my dream job aside from actually writing my own comics. Or even better, owning a comic book shop that also sold my work. My friends and I would run it together, doing what we loved.

"I keep asking Mr. Reynolds to hire you, to bring on more staff, but he won't do it," he said. "Besides, you won't be here much longer anyway. In just a few months you'll be off to art school."

"Yeah, I'm not so sure about that," I said.

"What do you mean you're not sure? What's up? Did they rescind your application or something?"

"No, I'm accepted and everything," I said. "But I still haven't come up with all the money I need for tuition."

"Oh man," he said.

"Yeah." I shrugged and handed him back the photograph. Dustin placed it back in the case and locked it. "So who knows. Unless I can somehow miraculously find twenty thousand dollars between now and August, or if one of these scholarships will come through, I don't have enough to pay for classes."

"They'll come through," he said. Dustin was ever the optimist, the one person in our friend group who always had a rosy disposition on things. "Even if they don't, you can always spend a year at GCC. That's what I'm doing. Going to study business management and then open my own shop."

"I hope you're right." It wasn't that I thought I was better than community college. I had taken a couple of dual credit classes there the last two semesters of high school. But all I could think about was having to stay in Greenwood for forever, like my brother, living at home. A home that still didn't feel like *home*. It was just a house, a place we lived in after...

I shuddered at the imagined worst-case scenario.

The front door bell dinged and we both turned. Hannah came in and someone else with her. She looked a bit like Hannah, with the same almond-shaped eyes and jet-black hair cut at her shoulders. There was a bright strip of pink in her bangs. She wore ripped jeans with Doc Martens.

"Hey guys," Hannah said. She walked up to the checkout counter. "How's it going?"

"Just showing Josh the newest Star Wars stuff," he said, gesturing to the glass cabinet.

The other girl remained silent but looked around, her

eyes taking in all the comics and collectibles. "This place is really cool," she finally said.

"This is my cousin Katie," Hannah said. "She's in from Chicago for a few weeks before college."

I tried not to stare, to say something, to introduce myself, but I was rendered silent.

"That's cool," Dustin said. He introduced himself and then turned to me, expecting me to do the same.

"Hi," I said. "I..." I stammered and eventually told her my name, which took more effort than it should because 1) talking to girls was never my strong suit and 2) this particular girl was gorgeous.

Katie just nodded and turned to the new comics shelf. "You guys carry all sorts of stuff. That's cool."

"You're into comics?" Dustin asked.

"Yeah," she looked up from the shelf of Image and Dark Horse books, flipping through the newest issue of *Spawn*.

"That's awesome." Dustin turned to me. "Josh is a comic artist. In fact, he's been accepted to the Indianapolis School of Art."

He turned to me, a sly look across his brows and I knew what he was trying to do. My cheeks burned.

"It's nothing really," I said. "I just draw some...stuff."

"You draw...stuff?" Katie looked at me now, her eyebrows lifted.

"Yeah." I gulped.

"Hey," Hannah said. "You guys are still coming over tonight, right?"

Saturday night was D&D night at Joel's house. Even if we didn't end up playing, we still spent every Saturday hanging out together.

"Yeah," Dustin said. "At least I think so. I haven't talked Joel today."

"We just left the pizza shop and walked over here," Hannah said. "Katie's going to come tonight, too. She's never played D&D." She gave me a quizzical look.

Dustin then looked to me as if I had the final say, which I didn't know why. I wasn't the Dungeon Master for this campaign, Joel was.

"Uh," I started. "Yeah, yeah, that's cool. Yeah, we can...yeah."

God, I felt like an idiot.

"Great," Hannah said. "Well, we just wanted to stop by and say hi. I'm going to take her to a few more places, see the sights. Show her all that Greenwood has to offer."

We told them bye as Hannah and her cousin Katie left, the door dinging again as they walked out.

"We're going to work on that," Dustin said.

"What?"

"How you turn into an absolute vegetable around cute girls."

I turned red again and walked back over the counter, taking a seat at one of the stools in front of it.

He was right. I had a lot of things to work on, but girls was probably lowest on the priority list right now.

CHAPTER 4

The four of us had the same D&D campaign going since we were in middle school. Hannah came around later when she and Joel started dating. But still, I always thought that was a pretty cool thing to brag about. Sure, a few other people had come and gone, but the core four was always there.

Tonight was no different, except we did have an extra person: Katie, who sat across from me at the folding table that we played at.

I let her borrow a set of dice from my bag and we spent an hour before playing helping her craft up her character. She had chosen a halfling rogue, a hobbit-like character, whom she lovingly called *little thieving bastard.*

As the evening wore on, I found myself more comfortable around her and we talked about the ways our high school experience had been different and the ways it was the same. It always seemed to me that no matter where you were from, some things remained universal. The cliques, the stereotypical athlete-jocks who ran the place, the pretty homecoming queens.

After a few hours, Joel, standing from behind his dungeon master screen, a cardboard trifold that hid his stats and game information, left us on a cliffhanger, our characters taken hostage in a castle.

"Whoa!" Dustin argued. "You can't do that." He pointed to Katie. "She won't be with us next time. How can you just leave us all tied up in the castle's jail like that?"

"Don't worry," Joel said. He lowered his face and gave us all a mischievous grin. "I have a plan."

"Well you better," Dustin said, crossing his arms. "We've only got a few more months to wrap this up anyway."

Joel gave me a knowing look that it was because of me that our campaigns were coming to an end. At least regular ones like this. I could still come back during holidays and breaks, but even I knew that wouldn't be the same. It's like a long-distance relationship. You say you're going to make it work at first, only to lose interest. But what do I know about long-distance relationships? I've never had a regular distance relationship.

"That was fun," Katie spoke up. "I can't believe you guys have been doing this for five years."

"Six," Dustin corrected. "Hannah came around a bit later, but yeah. We've been doing this every Saturday night since middle school."

"Geez dude, don't make us sound like even bigger nerds than we actually are," Joel said with an eye-roll.

"What?" Dustin said. "It's a point of pride!"

"I think it's really cool," Katie said. She then stood up from the table and pulled her bag over her shoulder. "Do any of you guys smoke?"

We all looked at each other, shaking our heads.

My brother smoked occasionally, despite our mom's protests. I thought it was something he did to fit in with the guys he worked with at the tire shop.

"Oh well," she said. "I'm going outside for a smoke then."

Hannah gave me a look, sort of gesturing toward the door with her eyebrows and I didn't have any problem interpreting it for what it meant. I may have been a nerd but not a social pariah.

"I'll join you," I said, a little quicker than cool. "If that's alright."

"Yeah, sure."

I stood up and followed Katie out the door that led to the deck of the apartment, glancing back at the table of my friends who were giving me thumbs-up signs.

Once outside, the warm night air was a nice reprieve from the stuffiness of Joel's place. It was a fun hangout, but as an efficiency apartment, it could get a little crowded with all of us in there. There was a slight breeze out of the northwest and you could almost smell the water from the Great Lakes.

Katie had already pulled a cigarette from her bag and was lighting it. She took a puff, blowing it into the air. "I've been trying to quit," she said, almost guiltily. "I used to hang out with some girls that tried to do everything we could to seem cooler than each other. This is the one bad habit that stuck."

"Yeah," I said, mostly because I didn't know what else to say.

"You want one?"

"No," I said, again too quickly to even seem remotely cool. "I never, I mean, I don't—"

"It's okay," she said, taking another puff. "And you shouldn't start anyway."

"How long are you in town?" I asked.

"For about a week. I used to come every summer, back when we were kids. But then when our—mine and Hannah's—grandma died, I didn't for a long time. And after graduating, I thought it would be fun to come back for a few days before starting college."

"That's cool." These words came out of my mouth because I really didn't know what else to say. Katie didn't seem to mind talking, and I didn't mind letting her steer the conversation. "Where are you going?" I asked. "For school, I mean."

"Purdue," she said. "I want to major in talent management."

"Like a sports agent?" I asked.

"Not quite, but something like that. More literary I guess you could say."

"That's cool," I said, repeating myself. I knew I

sounded like a broken record, but I didn't know what else to say or how to respond. She seemed so much cooler than me in every way. Even the way she smoked, it was like how you imagined someone in a movie doing it, with grace and ease.

"Look, Josh," she said, turning to me. "I think you're pretty cool, at least from today, and I'm sure you're nice and sweet and all that, but." She paused, taking another drag from her cigarette, the red cherry end burning brightly in the darkness. "You probably know that Hannah is trying to set us up."

"What?" I said. "No, I'm sorry, I didn't know at all. Is that what this is? Is that why you're here tonight?"

"But I'm just not looking for anything like that right now. I'm starting school in the fall in a new city, and I don't want to settle down or get into a relationship."

She said all this without acknowledging my question, which again, I didn't mind. If Hannah really was trying to set us up, I wish I had been in on the plan. Of course, there was most likely a reason I wasn't.

"Yeah," I said. "No, yeah, I totally get it. Yeah, I'm not looking for a relationship either. Gotta keep my options open, you know?"

She blew another cloud of nicotine smoke. "I'm glad you understand."

"We'll both be in Indy in the fall," I said. "That's kind of cool."

"Oh yeah," she said. "I didn't even realize that. Yeah, that is cool. How long have you been drawing?"

"For as long as I could hold a crayon, I guess," I said. "You know what? Can I have one of those?" I gestured to the cigarette between her fingers.

"Are you sure?"

"Yeah," I said.

She was hesitant, but then produced the box from her bag again and offered me a cigarette from its hold.

I lit it, not quite knowing how and took a puff, holding it between my thumb and forefinger, mimicking the way she did, and as I took a drag, I choked on the harsh smoke in my throat.

"It's a terrible habit to start," she said. "I'm going to be very upset if it's one you pick up."

"One doesn't make a habit."

She shrugged.

After a few more puffs, I didn't feel the sting as harshly. "But yeah," I said. "I've been drawing for a long time. I'm working on my own comic book right now."

Her eyebrows went up in interest.

"A comic book?"

"Yeah," I said.

"What's it about?"

"It's just," I started, not knowing really how to describe my book. I'd been working on it for years, rewriting it and redrawing it several times. "It's sort of a sci-fi story about, like, the Holy Grail in space. This spaceship crew is looking for it and chased by pirates and this evil guy who wants to use the Holy Grail to power his armies to take over the galaxy."

"That sounds really cool actually," Katie said.

"Thanks." I was never good at describing my own work, but her reaction and enthusiasm sounded genuine. It made me more confident. "The Holy Grail was what caused the Big Bang, you see, and it still has the power of the whole universe in it. You can create or destroy entire stars with it, entire planets."

"You'll have to let me know when you're done. I'd love to read it."

"You're into comic books?" Back at Galaxy, she had flipped through a couple, but it seemed more out of curiosity than being a reader. Still, I could feel the heat in my cheeks, the flutter in my chest at the idea that Katie, this girl, was into the things *I* was into. It didn't happen very often. I knew that the things that interested me were more like girl repellants.

"Sort of," she said.

"Have you ever read *The Walking Dead*?" I had recently discovered the series, and it changed the way I thought about writing characters in a graphic novel.

"Oh yes. It's so gritty. I like it a lot actually. My uncle gave me a bunch of his books that he'd read last year and I read through them all," she said. "It was part of my Senior Literature assignment. I wrote about how American graphic novels are just as important to literature as regular books." She took another drag from her cigarette, the thing getting close to the filter and she tapped the ash into the night air. I did the same, mimicking every move as if to say *look, I'm cool too.*

Katie continued, "I didn't know comic books could be like that, you know? Like, when I was little, I always had it in my head that comic books were just dudes in their underwear flying around fighting bad guys. But then my uncle showed me some of the new stuff coming out. I didn't know they could be so..."

"So heavy?" I finished.

"Yeah," she said, looking at me. Her eyes belied something there, and it made me feel that she had the same butterflies in her stomach that I had in mind, despite protesting differently. "Heavy. I like that."

"Thanks."

She flicked the end of her cigarette to the ground below. I could see it bounce in the dirt, the red ashes flickering out. I followed suit, trying to flick it with the same composure and coolness that she did, but I did not have the practice that it took. It tumbled from my hand and landed in the dirt.

"I think me and Katie are going to head out," she said. "It's getting late."

I didn't know exactly what time it was, but since our D&D campaigns could last for three to four hours, I knew it was well after midnight.

"Yeah, me too," I said. I didn't know if it was the nicotine or the sudden realization that I had been going almost nonstop since early this morning, but I felt exhaustion coming on hard. With Sundays off from Kaleidoscoops, I knew I'd get to sleep in tomorrow morning.

"Thanks for hanging out with me," Katie said. "And for being understanding."

"Yeah," I said. "Thanks for hanging out with me. And the cigarette. We can just be friends."

We went back inside the apartment, my friends giving me suspicious glances, asking me with their eyes *well? Did you make a move?* I had not, they knew that, but I appreciated their optimism.

After saying my goodbyes and putting my game books and character sheet in my backpack, I went to my car.

Even as I knew how tired I was, I also knew that I would spend tomorrow doing what I wanted most: work on my comic book. To create something *heavy*, something that Katie would want to read.

CHAPTER 5

You never know when a day is going to change your life, when something happens and the universe spins in a certain way that shifts everything you know. That day wasn't Sunday.

I didn't get as much drawing done on Sunday as I would have liked, mostly because I was stressing about art school. With my mom out preparing her open houses and my brother at work, I sat in bed for most of the morning, my laptop in my lap and searching for any scholarships I may have overlooked. As I scrolled through the websites, nothing had changed. It was all the same thing, the same lists and the same requirements. In the grand scheme of things, twenty thousand dollars sounded both like an attainable amount of money and completely out of the realm of possibility.

Despite my anxiety about my tuition predicament, I had the house to myself most of the day, and it was nice to just relax without having anyone else around.

But Monday? Monday morning when I woke up, I had no idea what was about to happen. I had no idea that Dustin was going to devise a plan that would change our lives.

That he would find a miracle.

I went back to work Monday morning, and even though it was getting hot as actual summer inched closer every day, Mondays were still the slowest day of the week, which meant that Mr. Gilroy only scheduled a skeleton crew. Not that I didn't get along with my coworkers, but most of them were much younger than me, still sophomores and working their first job.

When I arrived for my shift and to open the store, Mr. Gilroy was already there.

"Josh, before you open, could you come into my office please?" The man's tone was neutral and I didn't know if I was in trouble or worse—if I would have to turn in my keys and be unemployed. Given the amount of money to make up for tuition, I needed every single dollar I could save.

I followed my boss into his office, a tiny little room in the back of the shop, past the stock room. There was a desk littered with papers and receipts, a desktop PC that had to be from the 90's. Another tiny monitor was set up in the corner with the four security camera feeds on its screen. I sat in the only other chair available in the cramped space.

"Josh," he started, leaning back in his chair. Mr. Gilroy was in his fifties, maybe older—I never really asked. He had a cul-de-sac of hair that had grown grayer over the last couple of years that I'd worked here. "You've been here, what? Two? Three years?"

"This is my third year," I said.

"What do you plan on doing after your time at Kaleidoscoops is done?"

I didn't know how to answer the question. Was he asking me to quit? "I don't know what you mean," I said. "I plan on going to college."

"I see," he said. "Well as you know, Jessica left back in December and I've been trying to find her replacement."

Jessica was a few years older than me, and had been the store manager for as long as I'd worked there. But after finishing her associates degree at GCC, she'd gone on to work for a law firm as a paralegal. She left the purple apron behind and we'd not had a manager since, which I thought was more Mr. Gilroy not wanting to hire someone else and spend money on payroll.

Mr. Gilroy leaned forward now, clasping his hands in front of him. "I'd like for you to be my manager. It comes with a pay raise. A few more hours per week, of course, but you've been here the longest and I think you know the business well."

"I," I started, not really knowing how to react. "Thank you," I finally eeked out.

"So that's it then," Mr. Gilroy said. "There are a few things I will have to train you on over the next couple of months, mostly bank deposits and creating the schedule for the other employees, but I think you'll pick it up quickly."

I don't know if he could see my apprehension in my eyes, but I didn't feel accomplished. Despite what he said about the pay raise, it didn't feel like a promotion. Instead it was my worst fear. Would I be stuck living at home like Jake? Was this—scooping ice cream for the rest of my life—all there was for me? I was so close to getting to the art institute, it was so close to being in my grasp.

"Do I have to say yes today?" I finally said. "I mean, I appreciate it, I really do, but I just want to make sure I'm making the right decision."

He leaned back in his chair again, clicking his tongue in a way that insinuated that this wasn't the answer he was wanting. "I'd like an answer by the end of the week," he said. "I've got a lot of things in the works and I'd like to have my store manager before the next pay period begins."

"Okay," I said. "Thank you."

"Let's sell a lot of ice cream today," he said, dismissing me. He turned to the computer monitor that took up most of his desk, his attention now on some spreadsheet or order form.

I stood up, feeling uncertain but tried to maintain my poker face. "Yes sir."

I left his office not knowing that he would definitely have his answer by the end of the week—just not in any way either of us could anticipate.

I WAS HANDING a scoop of mint chocolate chip to a child with outstretched sticky hands when I looked up. There was movement at the door, a whirlwind of activity and motion. Dustin came in, almost running. He was out of breath as he came up to the counter, his hair floppy with sweat and over his eyes.

"You got a minute?" he asked.

"Um," I said, looking around. I spent the morning training my two coworkers that day, high school sophomores both of them, brand new to the job. Mr. Gilroy had left around lunch time and hadn't returned. That wasn't uncommon and as the senior member of the crew, I felt that I had some leeway. "Yeah, I might have a few minutes. What's up?"

"Not in here," he said. If I didn't know better, I would say that he'd actually sprinted the eight blocks from Galaxy Comics to Kaleidoscoops. His cheeks, usually pale, were red and sweat beaded on his brow, trickling down his temples in dirty streaks.

"What do you mean *not in here*?" I asked, the incredulity and confusion sure struck across my face. "Are you in trouble or something?" I leaned in and whispered, "Are the cops after you?"

"No, I'm not in trouble. Come on, I'll explain, but in private." He leaned in and I could smell the sweat on him. "It's the key to paying for your school. I've got a *plan*."

Dustin's plans, though optimistic and grandiose, rarely worked out but now I was curious. "Okay..." I said slowly. We had a lull in customers in the early afternoon, and I figured my two coworkers could handle anyone who came in.

"Hey guys," I said to them. They were both girls, gossiping together near the register. "I'm gonna step outside for a second. If you need me, come get me."

"Okay," one of them said. This was still her first week and I had not yet memorized her name.

"Alright, come outside," Dustin said.

I followed him out the door. The midday sun was high up above, the pavement hot and the wind blowing like a slow hair dryer. It was humid as well, the kind of weather that usually meant a good rainstorm would be in the forecast.

"This better be good," I said. I could already feel the sweat coalescing in my armpits, staining the white polo shirt beneath my apron. "You look like you're running from a crime scene."

"No," he said, "nothing like that." He leaned against the brick of the building, his knees shaking. "I think I've found something that..." he trailed off.

"What? Come on man, spit it out."

Finally, Dustin stood up straight, his eyes and body now resolute. "I've found it. I've found the holy grail."

CHAPTER 6

I HAVE TO ADMIT THAT I DIDN'T BELIEVE HIM AT first. I thought that Dustin was being hyperbolic and exaggerating the importance of what he'd found—well, *he* didn't even find it, as he later told us—and I was suspicious of it.

"Are you sure?" I asked.

"I am one hundred percent dead certain, dude," Dustin said. "This is it. This is a rocket-firing Boba Fett. And not just any rocket-firing Boba Fett. It's *the* rocket-firing Boba Fett."

He handed me the paper in his hand. It was a printout from a newspaper ad, an estate sale that had a huge collection of Star Wars memorabilia from the original movies. There were posters, toys, cereal bowls and action figures. And in the figures, a shot of them all laid out on a table in their retail packaging, was a grainy image of a Boba Fett.

"We need to get Joel," I said. "He's got that book, the *Complete Guide* or *Toy Archive* or something like that." I handed the paper back to Dustin. He folded it up and clutched it in his hand, refusing to let go of it or let it out of his sight.

"I already called him," he said. "He wants us to meet him at his place."

"Why?"

"Because, dude. We have to go get this thing."

"Dustin," I said, almost with a sigh. "We can't just leave and go and get a toy."

"Sure we can."

"Where even is this?" I asked, pointing to the paper in his hand.

"Agloe, Texas," he said, as if it was common knowledge.

"Where the hell is Agloe, Texas?" I asked.

"I don't know," he said. "I haven't looked it up yet. Look, what time do you get off work?"

"In an hour," I said.

"Perfect. Meet us at Joel's in an hour."

I looked up at the sky is exasperation. I could already tell this was going to be a *thing*. Dustin liked getting us into *things*. When we were in middle school, he wanted to sneak into a private screening of *The Phantom Menace*. Our sophomore year, he found which hotel Ewan McGregor was staying in for the comic convention in Indianapolis and wanted us to stake the place out to get an autograph.

"Josh," he said, pulling my attention back to him. "I know what you're thinking, that I'm going to try to lead you on some damned fool idealistic crusade. But this is the real deal. This is it. This is the key to paying for your art school."

AN HOUR LATER, after I'd shed my apron and cap and drove over to Joel's place, I climbed the stairs to his apartment over the garage. Given the vehicles parked out on the curb, I knew that Dustin and I weren't the only ones here.

I walked in to find my friends, along with Hannah and Katie, sitting at the game table, hunched over a book splayed out on the play surface. They crowded the thing, none of them greeting me until I was at the table with them.

"Oh!" Joel said. "Dude, have you seen this?" The printed newspaper photograph was next to the book, and they were all comparing both images.

"Yeah," I said. "Dustin showed me about an hour ago."

"This is insane," he continued. "There's only one of these in the world, and it's right here, at an estate sale."

"Just one?" I asked. "What do you mean? I thought they made at least a dozen of those Boba Fetts."

"Not like this one," Dustin said. "Check it out." He slid the book across the table's surface to me.

It was a copy of *The Star Wars Toy Archive*, and within its pages were hundreds of toys made over the last three decades, many from before we were even born.

I read the entry for *Rocket-firing Boba Fett* (*Prototype*). "Introduced through mail-in pre-order before *The Empire*

Strikes Back, the toy was eventually discontinued due to choking hazard from the rocket-firing mechanism," I read out loud.

"So here's the deal," Dustin said. He was much more calm now than he was an hour ago, when he'd literally ran from Galaxy Comics to Kaleidoscoops. "This toy was never released to the public. They stopped production on them and only exists in prototypes."

"And," Joel added, "only one was made and put in retail packaging. This one. They showed it off at a toy fair in New York in 1979." He picked up the printed paper that Dustin had brought. "This is the real deal, man. This is the king of action figures."

"This estate sale, they don't know what they have," Dustin continued excitedly. "They think it's just another toy like all the rest. But it's not. It's the only one that exists. And we're going to go buy it and sell it ourselves."

"Oh come on," I said. I grabbed the piece of paper that Dustin had printed off and read it over. The newspaper ad was grainy, but the information was clear. "How did you even find this?"

"Mr. Reynolds found it in the Sunday papers doing his online research over the weekend I guess. It was on his desk. I was putting the shipping labels together and saw it with the rest of his newspaper printouts. I told you, this is how he gets all the collectibles and memorabilia for the stores," Dustin said. "I saw this one and couldn't believe it. I made a photocopy and ran to find you immediately."

"You guys are acting like this thing is worth ten thousand dollars or something," I said.

Dustin leaned over the table and faced me like I was in an interrogation. "It's not worth ten thousand dollars," he said. "It's worth *a hundred thousand dollars.*"

Whatever sound tried to enter my ears from that moment stopped, replaced with a high-pitched buzzing as my brain tried to grapple with this information.

"Are you serious?" I finally asked.

"Dead serious," Dustin said.

I looked to Joel who nodded as well. I admittedly trusted his judgement more than Dustin's.

"This could change everything for us," Dustin said. "We get this figure, we drive down to Alco—"

"Agloe," Hannah corrected, who had remained mostly silent through the whole discussion.

"Right," Dustin said. "Whatever. Sorry. Agloe. Anyway, we drive to Agloe, Texas and we go buy this thing—and all the other toys—for two hundred dollars and we flip it. I mean, look at these pictures. Whoever this is, they have dozens of Star Wars toys in retail packaging from the seventies and eighties. They don't understand what they have."

"There's more than just the Boba Fett. If the prices in this book are right, there's a quarter million dollars in toys here, man. Even if we get half of what it's worth at auction, that's still twenty thousand dollars a piece," Joel said. "For all five of us."

"We would get to open our own comic book store," Dustin said.

"I could get my own place," Hannah said, leaning on Joel. "We could get an apartment together."

"And you," Joel added, looking directly at me, "you could afford your tuition. You could go to school and be a real comic book artist."

I brought my thumbnail to my teeth and gnawed at it. "You two are sure about this?"

"One hundred percent," Dustin said. "This is it. Like Joel said, this is the king of action figures, the ultimate Star Wars collectible."

I looked to Hannah, and to Katie, who stood beside her, emotionless and silent. "What do you two think?"

"I mean, I think it's crazy, but if he's right, it's even crazier not to go buy it," Hannah said. "That kind of money could buy us everything we've ever wanted."

"I think you're all nuts," Katie said. "But if I get twenty grand out of it, I'm in."

"Where even is this? Agloe? I've never even heard of it," I said.

"It's a little suburb just east of Houston." Dustin pulled a paper map of the United States from his backpack on the ground and unfolded it on the table. He had circled Greenwood and Agloe and traced the highway system between them in red ink.

"Jesus Christ, guys," I said, looking it over. "That's got to be a thousand miles."

"One thousand fourteen to be exact," Dustin said.

"And how are we getting there?" I asked. It was apparent to me that this was nothing more than a pipe dream, a crazy idea. Even if they were right about this Boba Fett action figure being this holy grail thing, it was too far, too much of a risk.

"My car is a shitbox," Dustin said. "And Joel's only has four seats."

"And my car," Hannah said, "is even more of a shitbox."

"So..." I said, the realization clicking in my head. "Mine. We take mine."

"Your Jeep has five seats and a ton of cargo space. It's a fifteen hour drive," Joel said. "We can sleep in the back if we need to, with the seats folded down."

"We could even take turns, driving in shifts. We could leave on Thursday after work and be there first thing Friday morning," Dustin said.

"I can't go this week. I have to work," I said.

"It's a hundred thousand dollars!" Dustin exclaimed. "Dude, listen to me."

I looked up at him.

"This is a once in a lifetime opportunity."

I stood up and paced in the tiny living space of the apartment. "I can't," I finally said. "I am up for manager at the store, I have more scholarship applications to fill out and hopefully get some money for school. This sounds great and everything, but I can't risk my future and my tuition on a fifteen hour roadtrip to buy some toy."

"This isn't just some some toy," Dustin said, the desperation thick in his words.

"Come on, man," Joel pleaded. "You have to believe us. This is real. Someone is going to buy this thing. They want just a little more than two hundred dollars for the whole lot, because they don't know what they have. But we do. This could change our lives."

"Or we get all the way down there and it's not what we think it is," I argued.

Dustin cut me off. "This *is* what we think it is."

I continued, "Or someone else gets to it before we do, and we've just wasted thirty hours of driving for nothing."

"That figure alone is a hundred thousand dollars," Hannah said. "Even if we sold it and got half that, it's still a lot of money."

I looked to Katie, who just shrugged her shoulders. "Don't look at me. Like I said, if I could potentially get twenty thousand dollars just for hanging out with you nerds, I'm in all day."

I sighed. "I'm sorry guys. I just can't."

With that, with their pleas that turned into silence, I left the apartment, walked down the stairs and got in my car. The car that my friends wanted me to drive two thousand miles, round trip, in the hopes of buying an action figure. I looked around the interior, at the seats and the cargo space, currently messy with work attire, books, and art supplies, trying to imagine all five of us in it for three full days.

I turned the ignition and drove home in silence.

CHAPTER 7

THAT NIGHT, I SAT IN BED, DOODLING AND THINKING about the action figure and my friends. The more I thought about it, the crazier this plan sounded. I had to give Mr. Gilroy my decision by the end of the week and I needed a plan—a *real* plan that didn't involve a fifteen hour road trip to buy an action figure that may not even be what we thought it was—to pay for the final portion of my tuition. All these things wrestled for space in my brain and my thoughts and I tried drowning them out in graphite on the paper.

Then there was also the thought that ate at the back of my head, the one that made me bite my fingernails with the anxiety of it: that perhaps my ambitions were too far out of reach, no matter how close it felt. That maybe being a famous graphic novelist was as much a pipe dream as finding some rare Star Wars figure and selling it for six figures.

As I sat there, there was a knock at my door, light

knuckles that could only be my mother's. Jake never even bothered, choosing instead to barge in if he ever needed anything.

"Come in," I announced.

The door opened and my mom stood in the frame.

"I was hoping you'd still be awake," she said. She was still dressed for work, a dark navy pantsuit and white blouse. Though it was professional dress, she still looked young, the only thing belying her age were the increasingly deep crows' feet lines at the corners of her eyes, the occasional grey hair among the strawberry blonde.

"Yeah," I said. I looked at my bedside clock, the red LCD numbers glowing bright in the low light of the lamp beside it. It was just after ten.

"Some more mail for you today," she said, holding a couple of envelopes out.

"From the school?" I asked.

"That's what they say."

I stood from the bed, placing my notebook where I'd been lying and took the envelopes from her.

There were two, one was from the financial aid office. I read it in silence, the contents reminding me that the balance of my tuition was due by August 15th, the week before classes started.

The second letter was another scholarship denial.

"Bad news?" my mom asked.

"Just the same, really."

"How much money do you need?"

"About eighteen thousand dollars," I said with a heavy

sigh. "I have twenty five hundred saved up, but it's nowhere near enough to pay the rest of my tuition. It's a little more than ten percent of what I need to be exact."

"I could always get a loan against the house," she said, shrugging as if it were that easy.

"No," I said. "I can't let you do that. You work too hard as it is. I don't know." I sighed and sat back down on the foot of my bed behind me. I knew that my mom had already pooled all the money she could to pay for my tuition. "Maybe this was just not realistic. Maybe I'm not meant to do this."

"That's not true and you know it," she said. "You are an incredible artist, you always have been. Ever since you were a little boy, you had a gift. You're meant to nurture that, to turn it into something, not just let it pass you by or give up on it just because of a hiccup in the plan."

I smiled at the little bit of positivity. "Thank you," I said. "I just feel stuck right now and I feel like I don't have much time to get *un*stuck. Every week, another scholarship turns me down, and I don't have very many weeks or scholarships left."

"It'll be alright. We'll figure something out," she said. She nodded to the notebook splayed out on the bed. "What are you working on?"

"Nothing really," I said. "Just doodling. Clearing my thoughts."

"Is it working?"

I laughed. "No, not really."

"Maybe you need to get out of your comfort zone," she said.

"What do you mean?"

"I mean you are here, or work or with your friends. Maybe you need to do something outside of your comfort zone, do something that scares you a little to shake up your thought process," she said.

"Yeah, but," I said. "Like *what*?"

"I don't know. That's for you to figure out. This is your last summer before you head off to college. Do something big, something fun. When I was a sophomore in college, I wanted nothing more than to follow Bon Jovi on tour all over the midwest."

"Did you?" I couldn't imagine my mom, who had been this professional real estate agent for my entire childhood, following a hair metal band across states, being a groupie.

"Well, no," she said. "I got pregnant with your brother that summer. Your dad and I married right after and moved out of the dorms and into the smallest apartment I had ever seen. But still, that doesn't mean that you have to just sit here and worry. At least enjoy yourself while trying to figure it out."

"Well, I'm not getting married or pregnant," I said.

She laughed, a full, hearty laugh that I had not heard in a long time. "That's a good thing. I'm going to bed. See you tomorrow," she said. She leaned in and kissed me on the cheek. "You've always been my baby. I still can't believe you're graduated and off to college. Crazy." Shutting the door behind her, I was left in my room in the silence again, the two letters from the school on my bed. My art book seemed to taunt me.

Instead of continuing to draw out of boredom and anxiety, I shut the book and put it in my nightstand drawer. I had to work in the morning and open the shop, which meant an early start.

Sleep came fitfully that night, and I tossed and turned. When I did actually doze off, I dreamed of Katie, smoking cigarettes and sitting in the passenger seat of my Cherokee. The road stretched on forever ahead of us. She was laughing, staring at me. I felt a stirring in my chest, my heartbeat rising with the excitement of it. Every time I reached out to take her hand in mine, she moved a little further away.

I didn't know what it meant—I'm not really into dream interpretations—but I knew it had something to do with the proposed roadtrip and my mom's advice. Would I look back on my life, twenty years from now, and regret that I didn't at least take a chance? That I tried to do everything safely, only to end up nowhere close to my dreams?

I LEANED against the cooler that held the twenty-five flavors of ice cream that we had available. Dark circles had formed beneath my eyes and I yawned incessantly.

"You feeling okay?" my coworker asked. She was new, hired for the summer. Her name tag said *Isabella*.

"Yeah, why?" I asked.

"I don't know. You just look...tired."

I laughed under my breath. "I am tired."

"Partying too much?"

I gave her a quizzical look. "Do I look like someone who parties hard?"

"Yeah, not really," she said with a shrug. She went back to the fountain drink machine, stocking the styrofoam cups in the spring-loaded holder. It was a slow morning for ice cream; we had seen only four customers all day and it was nearing noon.

Even the customers who did come in, I made their orders but my mind was elsewhere. I couldn't shake the feeling that maybe my friends were right. That maybe driving to Texas and buying a rare one-of-a-kind action figure was going to be the only way to ensure that I would go to the art school that so far seemed just out of reach.

More than that, I wondered if my mom was right too. That I was afraid to get out of my comfort zone. After what happened with my dad, I knew that I was afraid to take risks.

Greenwood, the school, the community, the ice cream shop, this was all I'd ever known. To leave that would be to take a risk. To look at the horizon of two setting suns, wondering what's beyond it.

CHAPTER 8

I HADN'T TALKED TO MY FRIENDS IN ALMOST TWO days, since the night that Dustin tried to convince me to drive a thousand miles for an action figure. Wednesday was new comic book release day though, and I knew I'd need to stop by Galaxy Comics to pick up my stack for the week. Ever since I'd discovered comic books—originally superheroes like the X-Men or Spider-Man, and then onto more diverse stuff that publishers like Dark Horse put out —I would save some money every week to buy a couple. It wasn't long afterward that I tried to create my own. Of course those first attempts were awful. I didn't understand the storytelling aspect of it, I just wanted to draw stuff that looked cool.

But in high school, that had changed. That's when I really put the narrative aspect of comic books with the art style. With Dustin and Joel's input, I wrote my first comic, a sixteen page sci-fi story based off the tale of Beowulf, which we'd been reading in literature class.

My friends loved it.

Our teacher, a curmudgeon named Mrs. Byers, took one look at it and scoffed.

But that was all it took. I was hooked, wanting to create and draw and write stories every spare moment I had. Even when I ran our Dungeons and Dragons campaigns, it became a way for me to workshop story elements, to see if they resonated with my friends.

Which was why this was so hard now. We'd done everything together for our entire adolescence, and all that was coming to an end, which made these last two days a sort of anguish that I wasn't expecting.

I knew that by disagreeing with them, by not jumping at the idea of driving to some unknown Texas town on the Gulf of Mexico, that I had somehow broken that bond and as I left Kaleidoscoops after my shift that day and drove over to Galaxy to pick up my week's comics, I had a bit of apprehension.

Still, I pulled up and walked into the shop, the bell above the door dinging as it always did, that comforting, familiar sound. There were a group of kids, probably early-teens, huddled at a table and playing Magic: the Gathering. In the large game room, there were a few more groups at table top games.

Dustin, though, was nowhere in sight. Instead, it was Mr. Reynolds, the owner of the shop, manning the checkout counter. I walked up to him, checking the aisles as I did, thinking Dustin would be around here somewhere.

"Can I help you?" Mr. Reynolds asked.

Like my boss, Mr. Gilroy, he was an older gentleman, but the similarities stopped there. Jeff Reynolds had long gray hair that he tied back in a ponytail and a goatee that was almost just as colorless. He was rail-thin and wore Star Trek t-shirts almost exclusively. His teeth, a set of dentures, were abnormally white and he smiled like a used car salesman. Today there was no smile as I walked into the store. He seemed more perturbed than anything.

"Yeah," I said, "I, uh, I'm here to pick up my holds."

The man sighed. "Last name."

"McCreary. Josh McCreary."

"Give me a second," he said, stepping off the barstool behind the checkout counter. "Let me go in the back and see if I can find your box."

He disappeared behind a curtain that hung in the doorway between the checkout counter and the stock room. I stood there for a few moments, feeling somewhat out of place. I was a regular here but I didn't recognize any of the people in the game room. They were all younger than me, maybe starting high school in the fall, spending their summer break with their friends, hanging out, playing games.

Just like Dustin and Joel and myself.

I wouldn't be the one to tell them that it would go too fast. That they would blink and then they'd graduate and these summer breaks would be no more. That they would be adults, with adult jobs like...managing an ice cream shop. I shook my head at the thought. That's what my life had come to.

Mr. Reynolds came back through the threshold, carrying a handful of comic books. He plopped them down on the counter. "These kids here never put anything in the right spot," he said under his breath. "Those look right?"

I glanced at the titles and nodded. "Yes sir."

The man sat back down on the barstool and punched at a calculator.

"That'll be $16.24," he said.

"Sixteen dollars?" I asked incredulously.

"And twenty-four cents."

"That's more than it was last month."

"I don't know what to tell you. Prices go up, kid."

I reached into my wallet and handed the man a twenty. He popped open the cash register and gave me my change without even so much as looking at me.

Then, he leaned over the checkout counter and yelled past me. "Okay, time's up. It's been an hour. Either pay up or head out."

Two boys playing Pokemon looked up like Reynolds was being ridiculous. One of them, a portly middle schooler with a mop of black hair, got up and handed Reynolds a wad of cash which he put into the register. The kid, his head held low like it was the last of his allowance, slowly walked back to the table where he was playing with his friend.

Under his breath, Mr. Reynolds muttered, "Kids think

this place is just a clubhouse, that the electricity and air conditioning is free or something."

"Is Dustin here today?" I asked, ignoring his complaints. "He usually works Wednesdays."

"Nope," the man said. "Called me this morning said he couldn't make it in. Some family emergency. Wouldn't be back for a few days. Left me having to deal with these... these ingrates."

My eyes went wide. "Oh," was all that would come out of my lips.

My friends were going to leave without me.

Fifteen minutes later, I pulled up to Joel's place. I stopped by Dustin's house first, but he wasn't home, which meant that he could only be here—that was if they hadn't left yet.

Both their cars were there, which gave me a sense of relief. I bounded up the steps to Joel's apartment and didn't even bother knocking on the door, just barged in.

Dustin and Joel were there, as well as Hannah and Katie. Dustin sat at the gaming table, his paper map unfurled and taking up almost the entire surface. Joel was stuffing clothes in a backpack while Hannah and Katie sat on the futon.

"What's up?" Joel said, a little confused.

"I just went by the comic store," I said. "Mr Reynolds said you had a family emergency," I said to Dustin, ignoring Joel. "I just needed to come by, you know, to make sure everything was okay." My tone was sardonic.

"Listen man," Dustin said. "We have to do this, and we have to leave today."

I let out a sigh. "Of course you do. I mean, it wouldn't be an adventure without some self-imposed hokey timeline, right? I should expect you two to cook up some *Raiders of the Lost Ark* business."

"No, you don't understand," Dustin said. He stood up straight. "Mr. Reynolds is flying to Texas Friday morning. I saw the itinerary. He's flying to Texas and he's going to buy the action figure. We have to get there before him."

"I was just there, at the store," I said. "He didn't look like someone who's about to take a weekend trip to Texas."

"That's because I called in today, threw him off. He was forced to work the store, and he wasn't expecting that. But I'm telling you. Yesterday, he had his airline tickets all printed up and everything. I saw it. He's flying out of Indianapolis early Friday morning and going to Houston. He's going to buy those action figures."

"So your plan is what? To drive down to Texas and beat him to it?" I said.

"Yeah," Dustin said.

"That's exactly what we're going to do," Joel added.

I stopped myself from rolling my eyes.

"We leave today, we drive as far as Memphis, maybe Little Rock," Dustin said. "Then tomorrow, we get up early and we get to Houston. We buy the stuff, we get back on the road and we are back home with the single most valuable action figure to ever exist before Mr. Reynolds even lands at the airport."

"You do realize that once he finds out, you're fired, right? You no longer have a job," I said.

"We're going to start our own store," Dustin said. "Hell, once we sell the Boba Fett, we could even buy Galaxy Comics if we wanted."

"Look, man," Joel said. "I know this freaks you out. It freaks me out a little too. But we *have* to do this. This is, like, a once in a lifetime thing. There's a hundred thousand dollars on the line—maybe more—and all we have to do is drive to Texas to get it."

"'All we have to do'," I repeated. "You sound like we're just driving up to Indy for the day to a comic con."

"Josh," Dustin said. He walked over to the main area and sat on the edge of the futon. "We're just as scared that this might not happen, but it's a risk we're willing to take."

A risk. I didn't like risks. The very thought made me bring my thumbnail to my teeth. I bit at it, this nervous tick that I couldn't stop.

I leaned against the door behind me. As much as I didn't want to admit, they were right. And I was scared. I was afraid that this wouldn't work out, that we would go on a thousand mile wild goose chase. But they were willing to make that decision. The risk of it invigorated them instead of paralyzed.

I then thought of my mom and her words. To do something that excited me. And as much as I hated to admit it, this was most likely going to be the only shot I had at making up the difference in what I owed in tuition and to follow my dreams.

"Fine," I said, almost inaudibly.

"What?" Dustin asked. He cocked his hand to his ear. "What was that? I don't think anyone heard you."

A smile formed across my lips as I gave in. "I said *fine.* Let me go home and grab some things. I'll be back in an hour."

Both Dustin and Joel cheered and high-fived each other and me. The girls sat on the futon and looked at us like we were ridiculous, jumping around the living room. My heart raced in my chest, the adrenaline of the decision already pumping through my blood.

This was it.

This was either going to completely change our lives or be the biggest mistake the five of us could collectively make.

CHAPTER 9

If Dustin was right, we would be gone for a couple of days, three at the most. I had no idea what to pack. With five of us, all bringing whatever we needed, I knew cargo space would be tight, so I stuffed my backpack with only a couple of t-shirts and an extra pair of pants. I grabbed my toothbrush and a stick of deodorant and shoved them in one of the side pockets.

We decided that if we had to spend the night somewhere, we could fold down the backseat and the three of us guys could sleep in the Jeep's cargo space. The two girls could push the front seats back and sleep there. In the garage, I rummaged around and grabbed a sleeping bag from our unused camping gear. We hadn't been camping in almost ten years, not since my dad used to take us.

I also grabbed my drawing supplies. I didn't know how much time I would have to draw, but at least it would help me alleviate my anxiety and give me something to do when someone else took a driving shift.

An hour later, I was back at Joel's place, back up the steps to his apartment and sitting in the living room while Dustin laid out his plan.

"How much money do we have? Altogether?" he asked. "I pulled two hundred from my sock drawer."

"I brought three hundred in cash with me," I said. I pulled the money from my college tuition savings and it pained me to do so. I was already so far away from paying the balance, and three hundred was still a huge chunk of what I had saved.

"I have three hundred," Hannah said.

"I also have two," Joel said.

"I only have a hundred bucks," Katie said, looking down at her feet.

"That's alright," Dustin said. "That's still a thousand dollars between us. More than enough for the Boba Fett."

Joel nodded. "We can split gas, we can eat cheap," he said. The biggest thing is the money for the action figures. The estate sale has the whole lot, forty figures total, for two fifty. We split that evenly, fifty for each of us, that will get it. Then we can sell the Boba Fett at an auction house."

"The other figures we can stock in our shop when we open it," Dustin said. "If that's alright with you guys." He looked to us, the girls and me, for our approval.

"Fine with me," I said. "As long as I get a discount on comics."

"Josh, if this works out, you'll never buy another comic book in your life," Joel said.

"Okay," Dustin said. "This is all perfect. We'll get to

Memphis tonight and if we can't find somewhere that feels safe to sleep in the car, we can find a cheap hotel to sleep in, one of those thirty-five dollar a night joints."

"Ew," Hannah interrupted. "And get bedbugs? I'll take my chances with sleeping in the car."

"It won't be that bad. But the important thing here is that we get to the people selling this stuff with as much money as we can," Dustin continued. "And as quickly as we can. So we'll get up early tomorrow and drive the rest of the way to Agloe. If we get there by early afternoon, we can get back on the road and be home Friday afternoon at the latest, rich as hell."

This all sounded too simple to me, but Dustin had obviously been thinking about this nonstop for the last few days, going over every detail in his head. For me, I couldn't stop thinking about everything that could go wrong. A wreck, a flat tire, a wrong exit that would take us somewhere far from our hopeful destination. I bit at the nail of my thumb, chewing on it.

I wasn't going to let my nervousness get in the way of this, I had determined. Even as I packed my things back home, talking to myself the entire time, I convinced myself that the *potential* here was worth more than any perceived error that I could conjure up.

Dustin shouldered his backpack, a black canvas bag. "Alright, what are we waiting for? Let's go get rich."

. . .

I DROVE THE FIRST LEG, with Joel in the passenger seat. He had the directions printed off from some map website. I knew how to get out of Greenwood, and I was pretty certain I knew how to get to Memphis, our first stop for the night.

Dustin sat in the back seat behind Joel, with Hannah in the middle. Katie sat directly behind me. As we turned out of Dustin's neighborhood, I caught a glimpse of her in the rearview mirror. She stared out the window, watching as we passed the houses and turned toward the highway.

"Obviously we have to get gas first before leaving town," I said.

"I packed some bottles of water," Hannah said, a plastic bag between her legs. "And a few other snacks that I could pilfer from the pantry in Joel's parents' house."

As we drove toward the gas station on the outskirts of town, we passed by my mom's office on Main Street.

"Actually," I said, slowing down, "I need to make one stop real quick."

I made a U-turn in Main Street and parked on the curb in front of my mom's office. It was, at one time, an old house that she and my aunt had gutted and converted into a real estate office.

"What are we doing here?" Hannah asked.

"This is my mom's office. I'll be right back." I put the Jeep in park and left it idling while I ran up the steps of the covered wooden porch, taking two at a time, to the front entrance. The door had a frosted glass panel, the original replaced with something that looked more professional and modern.

The inside of the office was a lot like that, too. The house had been completely renovated, the rooms widened and turned into offices, conference rooms, and even a break room. I spent many days after school when I was younger up there, doing homework in the conference room and raiding their refrigerator. My brother was usually at some sports practice after school, so I had the place, and my mom's attention, to myself.

"Hey Josh." My mom's secretary and personal assistant, Gwen, was a few years older than me and ran the front desk for the agency. She had been a senior when I was a freshman, and she had worked for my mom even when she was in high school. Her ebony hair was ironed straight and her bangs covered her eyebrows. I always thought she was really pretty, but to her I was still just a kid. When I was in elementary school, my mom didn't have a secretary. It was just her and my aunt.

"Hey Gwen, is my mom around?" I asked.

"Yeah, let me get her. Oh," she paused, holding the phone to her shoulder, "congratulations on graduation. Where are you headed?"

"What? Like right now?"

"No," she said slowly. "Like for college."

"Oh." My palms were already sweating. "Yeah, I'm going to the Indianapolis Art Institute."

"That's so cool. I remember that art show back when I

was at Greenwood High my senior year. You were, like, really talented."

"Yeah. Listen, I'm kind of in a hurry."

"Okay, yeah," Gwen said, "of course."

She dialed the three digit extension to my mom's office, which was converted from the master bedroom in the back of the house. I had learned to not barge in if she had clients back there with her.

Gwen said something into the receiver and then hung it up. "She said you can go on back."

"Thank you," I said. Walking down the short hallway, I passed by my aunt Cathy's office. Her door was closed, and I hadn't seen her car parked outside, so I was glad to know that I'd have a few moments of privacy with my mom.

I knocked on the open door. "Hey," I said.

"Hey! What are you doing here?" She gave me a once-over and her brows furrowed. "Are you alright? What's going on?"

"I just wanted to come by and let you know that I'm going out of town for a few days," I said.

Now her eyebrows went up in surprise. "Oh?"

"My friends and I," I said, "we're going to follow Bon Jovi on tour."

She laughed at this and crossed the room. She pulled me into a hug and patted me on the back. Pulling away, she said, "But seriously. Where are you going?"

"Agloe, Texas," I said.

"Where is that?" The question almost came out as a laugh.

"It's near Houston."

"You're driving a thousand miles? What for?"

"It's a long story, but I'll be safe, I promise. I'll call tonight."

"Good lord, Josh," she said. She walked over and leaned on her desk. "Nothing illegal I hope."

"No, nothing illegal," I said with a half-chuckle. "I swear, it's something I need to do. All of us, we need to do this before I head off to college."

"I think I would have preferred not knowing at all," she said. "I'm going to be a nervous wreck."

"I just needed you to know. I'm getting out of my comfort zone. You were right. This is my Bon Jovi, I think."

"Then," she said, and then with a smile, "get on the road. Do you need money?"

"No," I said. "We have enough. I hope."

"Well," she said, and I could tell she was still almost at a loss. "Just, be careful please."

"I love you."

"I love you, too. Call me whenever you can."

"I will," I said. "I'll be back Friday."

We hugged again and I went back out to my car.

"Everything alright?" Hannah asked.

"Yeah," I said. I put the vehicle in drive and went back onto Main Street. "Just had to let my mom know that I was leaving."

As we pulled onto the highway, driving south to Memphis, Dustin pulled out his CD binder from his backpack.

"Who is ready for some music?" he asked.

I looked at him through my rearview. "Got any Bon Jovi?"

CHAPTER 10

We had been driving for nearly three hours, following Interstate 70 through Indiana when I checked the fuel gauge, seeing that we were down to less than a quarter of a tank. It was getting dark, the sun setting faster every moment.

The first few hours of the trip were full of the joy of adventure. We listened to music, drove with the windows down, got big rig trucks to pull their air horn. After a while though we sort of settled into a more subdued atmosphere, talking about high school experiences and what we all wanted to do with the money that we were about to get.

"Hey guys," I announced, "we have to get gas."

"Already?" Hannah asked.

"Yeah, sorry. This thing is a guzzler." Just by quick calculation, I was getting twenty-two miles per gallon. A thousand miles there and back plus an extra hundred for a buffer, and with gas at just over two dollars per gallon, it would cost a little more than two hundred dollars total for the fuel for the trip. We just needed to ensure that we kept enough money to pay for food and—most importantly—the action figures in Agloe.

"We should stop and get some dinner, too," Dustin said. "I haven't eaten all day."

"I brought—" Hannah started, but Dustin cut her off.

"Yeah, I know. Hummus and trail mix and bird food. I'm talking about a big greasy burger and fries."

"I don't know, man," I said. "We should be frugal with our money."

"We brought plenty," he argued. "Besides, this is a road trip! The last one we're ever going to take together."

"Last I checked," Joel said, "it's the *only* one we've ever taken together."

"Even more important. Are we going to remember this as the trip that Hannah—you're a sweet girl and Joel is a lucky guy to have you—made us eat trail mix for three days straight or are we going to live it up and make memories that last forever?" Dustin was animated, hitting the shoulder pad of the driver's seat with his palm.

"You're going to remember a greasy hamburger for the rest of your life?" Joel asked sarcastically.

"Absolutely."

I looked to Katie in the rearview. "What do you think?"

"I'll go anywhere as long as I can smoke a cigarette in silence."

"That's not a no," Dustin said.

I sighed. "Fine. We just need to be smart with our

cash." I took the next exit for a town called Effingham. Following the frontage road off the interstate, I found a gas station, the large Conoco sign glowing in the twilight. The sun had almost completely set, which meant that by the time we ate and got back on the road it would be completely dark, pulling into Memphis close to midnight.

At the gas pump, I filled up the twenty gallon tank and paid inside. When I got back out, my friends had exited the vehicle, stretching their legs.

"Look," Dustin said, pointing to a building across the street. "Tune-Up Diner. That looks like the greasiest burger joint of all time."

I shrugged my shoulders. "I'll park the car and meet you guys over there."

They walked over to the diner while I found a vacant parking spot on the side of the Conoco station. When I turned off the car and got out, I found Katie leaning against the building, a cigarette glowing between her fingers.

"Having fun?" I asked.

"That backseat's a bit cramped," she said. "But yeah. You guys are cool."

"I can't believe we're doing this," I said. I brought my thumbnail to my teeth, chewing on the corner of it.

"That's a bad habit," she said with a drag of her cigarette.

"Something about a kettle and a black pot?"

This made her smile. "You're right. I shouldn't judge." She flicked the remains of her cigarette onto the asphalt.

"Let's go eat. And hope this burger is everything Dustin could ever dream of."

"I can't wait to write about it in my memoirs someday."

"Turn it into a comic book series," she said with a grin. "The search for the burger holy grail."

"You might be on to something," I said.

"I really would like to read your comic book sometime, you know."

"Really?" I asked. "Or are you just being nice?"

Looking both ways, we crossed the street to the diner's parking lot.

"I'm serious. I think it sounds really cool."

I did bring my art books with me, including the rough draft of the book. I brought my thumb to my teeth again and she smacked it down.

"Gotta keep those vices in check," Katie said.

"I will if you will."

I opened the door to the diner and she bumped me with her hip playfully. "Deal," she said.

IT WAS the best burger I'd ever had in my life. Whatever apprehension and disdain I'd had for the idea of stopping for a meal like this went out the window as soon as I saw the portions. French fries piled like mountains. Burgers dripping with grease. Milkshakes that made Kaleidoscoops taste like cardboard. Salt and sugar touched my tastebuds in ways that I'd only ever dreamed of.

"Holy shit," Dustin said, leaning back in the wooden booth. "That was amazing. Aren't you guys glad I made us stop?"

We all sat together in a booth in the back corner of the restaurant. Oldies music played over the ceiling-mounted speakers. It was the quintessential middle American diner, something out of an old magazine.

"You definitely found a gem," Joel said. "I think you earned some kudos for this one."

"I don't think I'll need to eat again for the entire trip," Hannah said.

"I mean," Katie said, "it was *okay*. Not the greatest in the world."

Hannah threw a French fry at her cousin, who playfully threw it back.

"Leave it to Katie to temper everyone's excitement," Dustin said.

"I didn't say it was bad, I'm just saying you guys are maybe over-inflating how good it is."

"We should get back on the road," I said, looking at the Timex on my wrist. As much as I enjoyed sitting here, all of us talking and laughing and discussing the life-changing action figure we were on our way to collect, the nagging in the back of my mind that we were already way off schedule wouldn't go away. "It's going to be well after midnight before we get to Memphis and we have to get started early tomorrow morning if we're going to get to Agloe before it gets too late."

"Fine, Dad," Dustin huffed.

The waitress, an elderly woman in a green dress and yellow apron, brought the ticket and we split the whole thing evenly, leaving a generous tip. A few minutes later, we walked back to my vehicle, piling back in.

"Alright," I said to Joel, who took the passenger seat. "Where do I need to go?"

He looked around nervously in the seat and shoved his hands in his pockets. Pulling all the contents out, he rifled through his belongings, eventually getting back out and looking around the floorboard.

"Uh," he finally said. "I can't find the Mapquest directions."

"Oh no," Hannah said.

Katie pursed her lips. "I've got a bad feeling about this," she said.

CHAPTER 11

"Guys, it's fine, I promise," Dustin said.

We all stood around the Cherokee, looking under the seats and on the ground around it.

"I'm telling you, I remember the way. I lined it out on that map, remember? We just stay on I-70 until it turns south," he said. "And then it's interstate all the way to Memphis."

"Maybe I dropped it in the diner," Joel said, ignoring Dustin.

"Let's go see," I said.

"It wouldn't hurt to at least check," Hannah said. Dustin started to argue again but she turned to him. "Look, I know you know the way, but I would feel better knowing that we had the printed directions."

"I don't know why you didn't just bring the map in the first place," I said to Dustin accusingly.

Dustin looked at the ground, kicked some pebbles with

the tip of his Chuck Taylors. "I forgot it," he said, almost inaudibly.

"How could you forget something as important as the map, Dustin?" Joel asked.

"How could you lose something so important as the Mapquest directions?" Dustin retorted. "We could do this all day."

"Look, guys," Hannah said. "Let's not argue. Katie and I will walk back over to the diner and see if the papers are in that booth."

While Joel, Dustin and I tore apart every square inch of the Cherokee's interior, the girls walked across the street.

"I feel so stupid," Joel said. "I had them folded up in my pocket. They must have fallen out when I got my wallet."

"It's alright guys, I promise. I remember the way," Dustin tried to convince us. "There's nothing to worry about. We're wasting time when we could already be back on the road."

"I don't know," I said. "I mean, I'm sure you do, but I know I would feel a lot better with the directions. And without a map, we can't even make a solid plan."

"That's your problem, Josh," Dustin said. "You always need some plan, some step-by-step guide for whatever you do. If you'd just let loose a little and not be so uptight, you'd understand that this is meant to be fun."

"Dude," Joel said. "Lay off a little, alright? Don't be a scruffy-lookin' nerf-herder."

Dustin stood up straight and held his arms out. "Who's scruffy lookin'? I'm just saying, it's not the end of the world."

I kept my mouth shut, not giving in to arguing about the situation. The truth was, it made me nervous as hell being this far from home without a map of how to get where we were going.

As we searched, I had even glanced over to the gas station where we'd fueled up, but the lights were out and the neon open sign powered off. This was a small town, so I wasn't surprised to see businesses close after 9pm.

As Joel and Dustin stood at the vehicle, I walked over to the gas station's front door's and peered inside, cupping my hands around my eyes. There was a spinning rack of maps, all folded and ready for purchase. The glass doors, framed with metal bars, were the only thing keeping me from the solace I wanted in this situation.

"Hey bud," Joel said as he came up behind me. "Sorry about him."

I stepped back from the door. "It's fine," I said. "He's probably right."

"I think—" he started, but I just walked back to the Jeep. I didn't want to hear his justification of Dustin's words.

The girls came back at the same time, both of their faces sullen. "Couldn't find it. The waitress said they'd bussed the table right after we left. If it had fallen out, it was in their garbage now," Hannah said.

Katie pulled a cigarette from her messenger bag, looked at me and put it back. I smiled.

"Look," Dustin said. "I know the way, I have studied it almost nonstop for three days now. I'll drive and get us to Memphis."

"No way," I started, but Joel put an arm across my chest.

"No," I continued. "You don't even have a map. You're just going to do this off memory? In the dark?"

Joel leaned into me. "Look man, let him do this. Take the backseat with Katie." He raised his eyebrows. "Fear is the path to the dark side."

Finally, I sighed and relented. "Fine."

"Alright," Dustin said, clapping his hands. "Everyone pile in and let's get back on the road."

I got in the backseat next to Katie.

"Why do I have the feeling," I said as I sat next to her, "that he is going to be the death of me?"

I WOKE UP, not realizing I had even dozed off. I was leaning against Katie's shoulder, my cheek nuzzled against her collarbone when I stirred. My eyes shot open and I immediately knew something was wrong. I could hear Dustin and Joel, in the front seats, quietly arguing back and forth.

"What's going on?" I asked.

"Uh, everything's perfectly alright here," Dustin said

nervously. "Just a slight...navigation malfunction. But we're all fine here. How are you?"

"Dustin," I said, almost growling. I look out the window. A city surrounded us, bright lights zooming by outside. "*Where are we?*"

"Uh," he said.

"Numbnuts over here took us to St. Louis," Joel said.

Hannah sat up now, poking through the space between the front seats.

"St. Louis?" she said. "You drove us to *St. Louis?*"

I sat back, leaned into the seat behind me. This could not be happening, I thought. But of course it was. Dustin, as cocky and self-assured as he was, had not known the way as well as he thought he had—or as well as he'd tried to convince us. My head started to pound, my temples radiating pain.

"Newsflash, jackass," Hannah said, still perturbed. "We are in Missouri. *Missouri* is not *Memphis.*"

"I know," he said. "I guess I missed the interstate exit at some point, I just don't know where," Dustin said. He was much less cocky now and he knew that, if only Hannah was the only one showing it, we were all upset.

"Just find a rest stop or something and pull over," I said, pinching the bridge of my nose. My head was starting to ache and my heart pounded nervously in my chest.

"I'm sorry," Dustin said, now much more sheepish than he'd been back in the parking lot at the diner. "I really thought I had the map memorized."

"Yeah, well, traveling through the interstates ain't like dusting crops, farm boy," Joel retorted.

Katie glanced over at me and even had a slight grin on her face, a sardonic look that belied the situation.

"What's so funny?" I asked.

"I mean, don't you find it at least somewhat humorous?" she almost whispered to me. "It's not a real roadtrip without some hijinks."

"I don't know if being lost in St. Louis counts as hijinks."

I kept my frustration about our current predicament to myself, choosing instead to stare out the window at the city's lights that twinkled and unfolded before us.

"What should we do?" Hannah asked.

"I don't know," Joel said.

"I say we just find a motel to stay at tonight," Katie said. "We can get our bearings in the morning, head out early and drive the rest of the way."

"I agree," Hannah said.

"All we need to do is just find a travel station," Dustin said, peering out through the windshield, looking at all the illuminated business signs. "They sell atlases, maps, stuff like that."

"Look man," I said, "it's almost midnight. I don't know how much more we can drive tonight anyway. I think Katie's right. Let's call it a night and head back out tomorrow when there's some sunlight."

"Look," Joel said, "there's a Motel 6."

Dustin took the next exit and pulled into the parking lot of the hotel. We all got out.

"Sign says fifty-nine dollars for the night, so twelve bucks a piece?" Dustin said.

I would gladly pay twelve dollars to get some sleep, to pass out and tackle the rest of the trip tomorrow.

Shit, I thought to myself. Tomorrow. I was supposed to work tomorrow, open the store and I completely forgot.

"I need to find a phone," I said. "I forgot that I'm scheduled to open the store tomorrow morning and I didn't tell Mr. Reynolds that I wouldn't be there."

"They usually have those in hotel rooms," Dustin said.

Together, the five of us walked into the lobby of the motel. It was a tiny room separated by the check-in counter. There were newsstands and racks of brochures. Maps of Missouri, but as I inspected them, nothing that would lead us to Houston.

"Can I help you all?" the woman manning the counter said. She looked at us through glasses as thick as magnifying lenses, making her eyes look huge.

"We need a room for the night. Two queen beds with a pullout mattress if possible," Dustin said.

"I need a credit card and a driver's license," the woman said.

"We, uh, we don't have a credit card," Dustin said, turning to us.

We all shrugged our shoulders. I had just turned eighteen right before graduation, so I didn't have a credit card.

By the looks my friends had on their faces, none of them did either.

Dustin turned back to the woman. "Can we just pay cash?"

"I'm sorry," she said. "You have to put a credit card on file in order to book a room. If you would like, you can pay with cash tomorrow at checkout."

"Ma'am," he said. "We're on a cross-country roadtrip. This is a once-in-a-lifetime experience and all we need is a place to sleep for the night. We're not going to make any trouble. We'll be out first thing in the morning." Then, he leaned on the counter, flashing the woman his most charming smile. The woman just gave him an exasperated look, her eyebrows like miniature arches. "Remember when you were young? Remember when you wanted to travel the country with your friends, do something exciting and life-altering? That's us, right now. So if you could have some mercy, show us a little grace and let us pay for the room tonight in cash, we would be forever in your debt."

The woman stood up from the chair behind the counter and leaned into Dustin. "I," she said, "didn't have any friends. Now, no credit card, no room. If you can't do that, then I have to ask you to leave. I'd hate to call the cops on what looks like a bunch of adolescent runaways."

Dustin sighed and shook his head.

"Come on," I said, "let's get out of here." I corralled my friends out the door.

As we walked out, Katie turned back. "Thanks for the

help," she said to the lady, a sarcastic smile across her lips. "You're a real hero."

We let the door shut behind us before the woman could respond.

Dustin handed me the keys, but I shoved them back to him. "You drive," I said. "I'm too..." I trailed off. I didn't know what I felt. Anger? Frustration? Exhaustion? Whatever it was, this whole deal just kept getting worse.

"I'm sorry," he said, leaning against the Jeep's driver door. We huddled around him as he stared at the ground. "I really thought I could get us to Memphis. I don't know what to do now."

He looked up at us, tears were welling in his eyes. For the first time this whole trip, he looked unsure, like we'd gotten into more trouble than we could handle. Which, we most likely were. We were three hundred miles from home, we didn't know where to go from here, and we had nowhere to stay.

CHAPTER 12

"There's got to be a travel station around here somewhere," Hannah said. "We can get our bearings there."

"Yeah," Dustin said, peering out the windshield, looking for any kind of exit. "I think you're right."

After leaving the Motel 6 on the edge of the city, we had been driving through St. Louis for almost ten minutes. There were lights all along the highway, but nothing looked like a safe place to stop.

On the right side of the road, I saw a sign lit up among the others. "Hey!" I said, pointing. "Take the next exit!"

There were signs for restaurants and hotels, retails shops and stores, but nothing else that looked like it could help us in the current moment except for the one that stood out: in bright blue and yellow neon, the sign said *Dagobah Comics*.

Dustin, weaving across three lanes of late-night traffic,

took the next exit and pulled into the minuscule parking lot in front of the building. It stood back from the rest of the shops and restaurants along the highway, the metal building almost hidden and off the road. Across the parking lot was a Howard Johnson hotel, which meant that these cars could be overflow parking. Still, the sign for the comic shop glowed bright like a beacon.

"Are they open?" Joel asked, peering out the window.

There was a collection of cars in the parking lot but there was no illuminated open sign to be seen.

"I guess we could go see," I said. "Hopefully there's someone here who can point us in the right direction."

We all got out of the car and walked to the front door of the building. The glass panels on either side of it were emblazoned with advertisements and vinyl graphics for new comic releases. The door was covered in frosted glass and we couldn't see anything inside, but there was light and I could almost hear a murmur of sound from inside.

Dustin pulled on the door, but it didn't budge.

"Shit," he said. "It's locked."

"It's almost midnight," I said. "They're probably closed."

"Do you guys know this place or something?" Katie asked.

"Dagobah was the planet in *Empire Strikes Back* where Luke found Yoda," I explained.

"Who?" she asked.

"You've literally never seen *Star Wars*, have you?" I asked.

She shrugged her shoulders.

"Hannah," I said, "are you sure you two are related?"

I turned back to the door and tried to peer through the frosted glass, my hands to my face like I had done at the station back where we'd lost the map. I couldn't make out anything inside, but there were definitely lights on.

I knew that Galaxy Comics held extended hours on the weekend for gamers to use the space to play trading card games like Pokemon or Magic: the Gathering and for Dungeons and Dragons groups to have a space to play their campaigns, but on a Wednesday night, they shut down around ten. I assumed this place was the same.

Still, the parking lot was almost full, and I swore I could hear commotion inside.

"Let's just find a gas station," Hannah said. "Fuel up, get a map and get out of here."

I agreed and we started back for the car when a slider in the middle of the door opened up.

"Who are you?" a gruff voice asked from behind the door. Bespectacled eyes were visible behind the slider.

"We're looking for some help," Joel said, turning back sharply. "Are you guys open?"

"Looking? Found someone you have, I would say," the voice said.

We all looked at each other, confused.

"Uh," Dustin said. "Yeah. Listen, we just need some help finding a gas station or something."

"Out-of-towners?" the man said.

"Yeah," we all answered.

"An event we are having," the voice said. "Open to the public we are not."

I shook my head. We didn't have time for games. We were way off course and needed to get back on the road.

"Look, sir," Katie said. "Can you help us or not?"

I appreciated her being straight to the point.

"Enter you may if this question you can answer," the man behind the door said.

I sighed. "This is ridiculous. Let's go."

"Wait," Dustin whispered to me, grabbing me by the arm. "I've got a good feeling about this."

"Oh boy," I said sarcastically.

"Just," he said, "hang on a second." Then he turned back to the door. "What's the question?"

"Who is the rightful owner of the Millennium Falcon?" the voice asked.

Dustin was about to answer when I put my hand on his shoulder. "Wait," I whispered. "It's a trick question." I turned to the door. "Can we take a moment to discuss this as a committee?"

"I am *not* a committee," Hannah quipped.

"A moment I will give you," the voice said.

I huddled with my friends. "Look guys," I said. "It's a trick question."

"What do you mean it's a trick question? Han Solo owns the *Falcon*." Dustin said.

"No," I said. "The answer is, *it's contentious*. Han Solo lays claim to the ship because he won it in a card game against Lando Calrissian. But Lando refers to it as *his* ship, inferring that Solo may not have been playing above table. Plus, in *Return of the Jedi*, Lando is given command of the *Falcon* by Han and we don't see it in Han's possession again. At least not in the films. So the answer is *it's contentious*."

"Han gave him command, but he still owns the ship," Joel said.

"*If* Solo was playing cards by the rules, which there's enough information in the films to infer that he wasn't. I'm telling you, this is the answer."

"Then," Dustin said, "you answer. If we're going to get any help here tonight, it seems like we'll only be let in by getting this right."

I looked to Hannah and Katie, hoping they'd have some insight. "Do you two have any suggestions?"

"Don't look to me for help," Katie said. "I don't even know what an aluminum falcon is."

My shoulders dropped, then I turned to the door.

"I have our answer," I announced.

"Hear it now, I will."

"The answer is: ownership of the ship known as the *Millennium Falcon* is contentious since it was won under dubious circumstances in a card game by Han Solo against Lando Calrissian. Both men lay claim to the ship, without it ever being clear on who actually owns it. Both men pilot it in the films."

The slider on the door shut.

"Well hell," I said. I turned back to my friends. "Let's just go."

Then, a latch unlocked and the door swung open behind me.

"Welcome," the man behind the door said, "to Dagobah Comics."

CHAPTER 13

We stepped inside and stood, almost in awe. There were comics lining the walls, merchandise and collectibles in glass cases. But in the middle of the store there were several tables lined up. Dozens of people were sitting at them, playing a card game.

"What is this?" I asked.

"This," the man said, shutting the door behind us, "is the largest collection of Star Wars Collectible Card Game players in the midwest."

He was short and portly, with a receding hairline that ended in a ponytail tied at the back of his head. His eyes were framed with glasses. His t-shirt, an image of Han Solo and Princess Leia embracing, stretched across his belly.

My brows furrowed. "The CCG was decommissioned three years ago," I said. The company that created the game had lost their license and Lucasfilm, the company that owned all things *Star Wars*, had awarded it to another, who created their own card game. The CCG though was the one that Dustin, Joel and I had bonded over in middle school.

"Which is why we have to have secret tournaments like this," the man said. "But the game is dying. The cards are getting hard to come by because our players have to buy them from third-party sellers. Those bastards at Wizards of the Coast don't want us in operation and are squeezing us out. But we've just made a deal to keep Wizards out of here forever."

"Who are you?" Katie asked. "And are you going to help us or not?"

"My name is Yoda," the man said.

We all stood, almost wide-eyed with shock. Then, to my surprise, laughed. All of us, giggling.

"No, seriously," Hannah said. "Who are you?"

The man did not crack a smile. "I am Yoda, and this is my store. My home this is."

I cleared my throat. "Look, here's the thing. We're on our way to Texas and were supposed to stop in Memphis overnight, but we took a wrong turn somewhere and ended up here. We need to find a place to stay tonight as well as a gas station or travel station to find a map so we can find our way to Houston by tomorrow."

"Houston?" Yoda said. "You're about twelve hours from Houston."

I groaned. "Great," I said.

"But, I'll tell you what. You play in my tournament and help you, I will."

I screwed my face. "That's it? Just play some cards?"

Yoda took a step towards me and squeezed my shoulder. "Well, and win of course." He pointed to a poster on the wall. It read *Monthly SWCCG Tournament Tonight. $50 buy-in.*

Fifty dollars was a lot of money, especially for what we had left. After gas and dinner, I had already spent fifty of the three hundred I'd brought with me. Another fifty was cutting hard into what we'd need not only for the action figure in Agloe but also for the trip home. "Win?" I asked. "What if I don't?"

"Then," he said, a grin spreading across his face. "I keep your ship."

"My ship?"

"Your car."

I gulped and stepped back. "No," I said. My face went hot with fear, the hair on the back of my neck standing on end. "No way." Then, turning to my friends, "Let's get out of here."

We all started for the door and pulled but it was locked.

"Oh, I'm afraid you and your friends will find that the lock is fully operational," Yoda said, with that same devious grin.

I stood up straight and gritted my teeth."I'll do it," I said. "I'll play your tournament and when I win, you'll give us what we need."

"No," Katie whispered beside me. "Don't do this."

"It's alright," I said. My blood boiled in my veins. "I can use my own deck?" I asked Yoda.

"I," he said slowly, "would have to approve the deck, but yes, I think that would be acceptable."

Then I turned to Dustin, who was checking out some cards on a nearby table, almost absent-mindedly at first, but then I saw something change in his demeanor. Yoda started over and tried to take them up before Dustin got too close.

"Wait, you can't—" the guy started.

Dustin had one of the cards in his hands and he turned it over, checking it out closer. On it was a photo of Han Solo, but it was like a still from the movie, grainy and hazy. "These aren't real," Dustin said.

"Of course they are," Yoda said, almost nervously.

"No, this card was never commissioned by Wizards of the Coast. I would know. I have them all."

The rest of us turned our gazes to Yoda. My eyes narrowed.

"What kind of game are you playing here?" I asked.

"You're making your own cards," Dustin said. "These are counterfeit."

Yoda's eyes were shifty as he looked from us to the room of players.

"That's what this is. It's not just some dead card game. You're making *new* product, aren't you? Unlicensed, counterfeit cards," Dustin pressed.

"Look," Yoda said, "do you know how much money this card game made me? When it was discontinued, I had to find something to keep it going. This tournament is a proving ground. It helps to see if the cards we make work in real play."

"This is illegal," I spat. "And you want us to play in your illegal game, to—what, exactly?"

"You have a deck outside of this store's inventory control. It will be a perfect opportunity to test your skill against my ingenuity. And if you win, I promise I'll help you get what you need."

I didn't know if we could trust Yoda, but I also didn't know what other choice we had. It was obvious there was only one way out of here—to play this game. I turned to Dustin. "You have your cards on you, right?" I asked.

"Always," he said.

"Good."

He reached around the backpack on his back and pulled out a deck box. He handed it to me.

"Though the odds of you winning with it are..." he started, but I cut him off.

"Hey," I said. "Never tell me the odds."

I turned to Yoda and nearly shoved the deck into his chest. "Here you go. Approve this and then let's get started."

Yoda took the cards from the box and inspected them. "This deck looks acceptable. You may play."

As Yoda led me to a table, I turned to my friends as they followed us. "This," I said, "is where the fun begins."

. . .

I HAD BEEN PLAYING for nearly three hours, beating three opponents easily, but I was getting exhausted and could feel my concentration slipping. On the table in front of me, there were nearly fifty cards laid out in different configurations, planets cards and character cards all in arrays.

The guy I was playing against, a sixteen year-old kid with unruly hair in tight curls, concentrated on the layout in front of us. Playing as the Dark Side, he had a Death Star card with both Emperor Palpatine and Tarkin on it.

Sweat dripped down my brow as I anticipated his next move. If he did what I thought he would—move his Death Star to attack my fleet—I had the ultimate counter.

He did. After a second of hesitation, he moved the Death Star. I threw down my Luke Skywalker and X-Wing squadron, which had enough battle points to destroy the Death Star and take out the Emperor.

"I win," I said, leaning back in my chair, exhaling with pride. My friends around me whooped and cheered. The rest of the attendees, other players who had been knocked out of the tournament, surrounded us in awe.

"No," my opponent scoffed under his breath. "That's not true. That's impossible!"

Yoda, who sat at the head of the table, stood from his chair. "We have a new champion!" he exclaimed.

I stood up too as my friends surrounded me with hugs. "We did it!" I said.

I turned back and shook my opponent's hand, who

started gathering his cards. I noticed more than a few of them looked counterfeit, having been made in this shop.

I gathered up my own cards, sliding them back into the deckbox that Dustin had provided. We had spent so many hours playing this game in the school library when we were in the seventh grade, building and curating our best decks. It felt good knowing all that time had paid off.

"Thanks," I said, handing him the box.

"Great shot, kid, that was one in a million," Dustin said, still beaming.

Then, I went over to Yoda whose face was downturned and upset.

"Okay," I said. "I won. Now you'll help us."

CHAPTER 14

Yoda came back from the back area with a folded map of the United States and a stack of other papers. As he dumped it all on the checkout counter, my friends and I looked at him with disbelief.

I picked up one of the papers. It was slightly larger than a dollar bill, printed on regular computer paper. It had Yoda's face emblazoned on it—this Yoda, not the real one.

"Yoda Bucks?" I said, holding one between my thumb and finger, reading it out loud. "The winnings are...Yoda Bucks?"

"Five hundred dollars of store credit, good for anything in stock," he said. "Except for collectibles in the glass case. Those are cash-only."

"You've got to be kidding me," I said. "We don't want or need store credit."

"Credits will do fine," Yoda interjected.

"No they won't. Only money. We're trying to get to Houston."

"Ah yes. That's why I have the map." He tapped his finger on the folded atlas. "This will show you the way."

"Come on," Joel said, tugging at my sleeve. "Let's just get out of here."

I didn't trust Yoda, and after he suggested that he'd take my car if I didn't win the tournament, I wasn't too keen on being around here much longer either. Still, I took the map and unfolded it on the counter. The creases from the folds were deep, but it was clearly legible.

"At least this is something," I said. "Why do you even have this?"

"I have to travel a lot for gaming and comic conventions," he said. "It's important to know where you're going."

That made sense to me.

"Thanks for playing in my tournament. You kids are welcome back anytime." He flashed a smile, knowing that he wasn't out much since we weren't going to use his Yoda Bucks.

I just huffed at the remark. Somewhat dejected, my friends and I turned for the door to head out and get back on the road, to find some parking lot somewhere to spend the night in. At the last second, a thought pinged in my mind. I stopped in the doorway and turned back to Yoda. I was feeling confident and the adrenaline from winning the tournament hadn't left my body.

"Actually," I said, "there's one more thing you can do for us."

"What is that?" he asked, his eyes darting around.

"Do you have a credit card, Yoda?" I asked.

The man just looked at me, confused.

"You see, we need a hotel room for the night, and there just happens to be a hotel right across the street. A nice one too, with soft beds and free continental breakfast. We need you to put your card on file for us so we can stay there. We'll be out first thing in the morning," I said.

I could hear my friends behind me murmuring, and I knew it was a bold ask, but again, I had just beaten the man at his own tournament.

"No way," he said. "You won the tournament and I gave you the map. Anything else wasn't part of the deal."

"I'm altering the deal. Pray I don't alter it any further," I said. "I'd hate to get the authorities involved in this little illegal operation you've got going on here. I'm sure Wizards of the Coast would love to know that you're running an illicit game with an unlicensed Lucasfilm product."

He stood silent for a moment, laser beams almost shooting out of his eyes. Finally, he averted his gaze.

"I'll tell you what," I said. "You keep the store credits; you just get us a room at the HoJo across the parking lot and we'll swear to secrecy on this operation."

"And you're gone first thing in the morning?"

"Yes."

"And you stay silent about my shop?"

"Yes."

He looked to my friends who all made the same promise.

"Fine," he relented. Going back around the checkout counter, he picked up the telephone.

"Hi, I'd like to book a room for the night," he said into the receiver. "Yes, I have my card ready."

WE DROPPED our bags in the room. It was well after two in the morning, and I knew we'd have to get on the road by no later than nine if we were going to get to Agloe in time to buy the action figure before the estate sale opened on Friday. We were already well behind schedule but we all needed a place to crash for the night in order to get going again tomorrow.

"I can't believe you got us this," Dustin said, patting me on the back.

I couldn't either. I was certain that we'd be sleeping on the side of the road, all of us sharing the cramped space of the Cherokee. Instead, we'd get a chance to get some real rest, even if just for six hours.

Joel and Hannah took one of the queen-sized beds, which left the other sleeping arrangements kind of awkward. Though the pullout mattress tucked in a loveseat in the corner would probably be less comfortable than the actual beds, it meant that Katie would have to share the second queen with one of either Dustin or myself. She saved us any real argument by offering to take the foldaway.

We all took turns brushing our teeth and changing out of our clothes. Though it was so late, I was still too worked up to fall asleep. I slipped out of the room with the excuse that I was going to the front desk to get some toothpaste.

Instead, I went to find a payphone.

"Hi," I asked the person working the check-in area. He was a young person, probably not much older than me. His work attire, black slacks and a white button-up, hung awkwardly on his boyish frame, like a kid playing dress-up. "Is there a payphone somewhere?"

"There's one in the hallway, just across from the fitness center," he said, pointing in the direction of said hallway.

I went down the hall and found the payphone, hanging on the wall with a sort of wooden divider around it for some semblance of privacy. Taking some quarters out of my pocket, I dialed the number to Kaleidoscoops. I knew no one would be there but that the answering machine would get it.

The phone rang and the answering machine eventually did kick in. After the after-hours message, the machine beeped.

"Hi Mr. Gilroy, it's me, Josh. Listen, I'm so sorry but something has come up and I won't be coming in today. I know this is extremely last-minute notice, but I'm out of town. I won't be back til probably Saturday. Anyway, thank you and I'll see you later. I'm sorry again. Okay, bye."

I hung the receiver back in its hanging cradle and stared at it for a moment as it swayed in place. A pang of regret washed over me for a moment as I knew that I'd left my boss and my coworkers hanging as well. So much of my future hung in the balance of this roadtrip and the end result.

Instead of going back up to the room, I walked outside, out the back of the hotel, where there was a courtyard that looked out onto the river. The water was dark, sparkling under the lights of the city. Off in the distance, I could see the Arch, the great monument of the midwest.

Finding a bench in the courtyard, I sat down and stared at it.

So much had happened in the last twenty-four hours and we were nowhere near even half the way to our destination. We had so much driving yet to do and, after looking at the map and calculating the distance, it would take us nearly twelve hours of straight driving to get there.

I heard some rustling behind me, the door opening quietly. I turned to see who it was and was pleasantly surprised to see Katie coming out.

"There you are," she said. "What are you doing out here?"

"I don't think I can quite go to sleep," I said. "That tournament got me all riled up."

"Yeah, I know what you mean." She pulled out her cigarettes, putting one between her lips. "Want one?" she asked. "I know, I know, kettle and pot. But it helps me relax. Just this once."

"Yeah, I guess so." I didn't know if it would help me relax, but it was something to take my mind off of everything else. She handed me a cigarette and the lighter. I lit it and took that first puff. It still stung my lungs, but it was a welcome feeling.

"That's really pretty," Katie said, gesturing to the arch.

"I have never seen it before," I said. "All through my childhood, when my brother and I were little, my parents always talked about some cross-country roadtrip vacation that we would someday take. It was always *someday*. Someday we'll go to Yellowstone. Someday we'll go to Disneyland. Now here I am, graduated and off to college, and the most we ever did was went to Cedar Point, the *roller coaster capital of the world*. That was before..." I trailed off. I didn't like to talk about what happened.

"So you thought the arch would be better than a rollercoaster theme park?"

I laughed. "No. I mean, it's really cool. I guess I just feel like I missed out on something. What that is, I don't know." I took another drag from the cigarette, mimicking Katie as she did the same. "What about you? Have you ever been to St. Louis before?"

"Yeah," she said. "My dad lived here for a while when I was little."

"Oh wow," I said. "Where does he live now?"

"I have no idea."

"Oh." I looked at her, sitting next to me. Her face was expressionless as she stared at the arch.

"It's okay. He and my mom divorced when I was really little. We had a lot of contact for the first few years, into middle school. But then we drifted apart. I don't know, I guess he just didn't know how to be a dad," she said.

"Still," I said. "I'm sorry."

"It's okay. The week-long visits became less and less frequent, and then evolved to just phone calls that eventually stopped as well. I got a Christmas card from him when I was a freshman, the return address was somewhere in Arizona. That was the last I heard from him."

"Jesus," I said. "That's..." I trailed off. I had an excuse for my dad not being around anymore.

"I don't even know why I'm telling you all this."

"I'm glad you did," I said. "I mean, I'm not glad that that happened, but that you feel safe to share it with me. I don't know what I'm saying. I'm rambling. I'm sorry."

I gave her a slight smile. I didn't know why either, but in that moment, that's all I wanted—to share everything about each other.

"Thank you for getting us this hotel," she said. "That took some real balls."

"It was a long shot, but I felt like taking a risk," I said.

"Well done."

"Thanks."

"How long do you plan on staying out here?" Katie asked.

The real answer was *not very long*. I was starting to

feel the exhaustion of the roadtrip. "As long as you want to," I said instead.

She smiled and then did something I didn't expect: Katie scooted a little closer to me and rested her head on my shoulder. My heart raced with the physical touch. Her jet-black hair smelled like vanilla and smoke.

"You're not so bad, Josh," she said. "A little nervous, but pretty cool."

"I can promise you," I said, almost chuckling, "no girl has ever accused me of being cool."

"That's too bad, because you most definitely are."

We sat like that for a few minutes longer that seemed to stretch for forever. We watched as a container ship sailed past slowly down the river.

Katie rested her head on my shoulder for so long that I finally looked over to see that she was asleep.

"Hey," I whispered, nudging her.

She stirred awake. "Shit," she said. "Did I fall asleep?"

"Maybe for a minute or two. Let's head back in."

She agreed and, holding the entrance for her, we walked back up to our room on the third floor. I quietly opened the door with the electric keycard and almost tip-toed in the darkness of the room. A little light filtered through the window, and as my eyes adjusted to it, I was able to see that Dustin had passed out on the foldaway bed.

"It's okay," Katie whispered when she saw him there. "You can sleep with me on the bed."

"Are you sure? I can sleep on the floor, I don't mind."

"Don't be ridiculous," she said. "Come on, let's get some sleep."

I crawled into bed next to her, sleeping in my clothes. I fell asleep quickly, dreams of rollercoasters in my head. And on those rollercoasters, Katie was next to me, her head on my shoulder.

CHAPTER 15

I WOKE UP THE NEXT MORNING TO THE PHONE ringing in our room. The sound scared me as I shot up, not knowing what it was, coming out of sleep delirious and still exhausted.

"Somebody turn off their alarm," Joel mumbled from the other bed.

I reached for the receiver on the telephone that sat on the bedside table between the two beds.

"Hello?" I mumbled.

"Is this Mr. McCreary?" a voice said.

"Uh," I said. "Yes? Who is this?"

"This is the front desk. We got a phone call for you from a Thomas Gilroy. May I patch him through?"

My heart sank in my chest and I was immediately awake, the deliriousness of lack of sleep leaving, replaced with a queasy nervousness.

"Uh," I said. "Yeah."

There was a click and then I heard Mr. Gilroy's voice. "Josh?"

"Hi Mr. Gilroy. I take it you got my message."

"Where *are* you?" Mr. Gilroy didn't sound very happy.

"Well, where did you call?" I said.

"Not funny, Josh. How am I supposed to run this store with no notice from my potential manager?"

"I'm sorry, it was a last-minute thing. I literally had no access to a phone until late last night. But like I said, I'll be back to work my shift on Saturday." I was trying to be calm and polite but Mr. Gilroy's hostility made my chest tight. I had just graduated high school, I had never called in to work for anything and here I was, feeling like I was tied to this job at an ice cream shop.

"This is incredibly disrespectful and self-centered. I depend on you. I was going to make you my manager, but —"

"Was?" I said, cutting him off.

"That's right. *Was*. I don't know that I can make that decision now. I don't know that I can have someone who's just going to skip town at a moment's notice my manager. I was depending on you to be more mature."

Katie stirred in the bed next to me and rolled over, still asleep. I held the phone a little closer to my mouth and spoke quietly so as not to wake her, or the rest of my friends.

"Well then," I said into the phone. "Let me make that decision easy for you. I quit. I don't want to work at an ice cream store for minimum wage for the rest of my life. So I guess you're just going to have to figure it out." I hung up the receiver, which felt better than it should. At the same time, the weight of my words hit me and my stomach dropped.

"Wow," I heard Dustin whisper from the foldaway bed. "You are braver than I thought."

His voice startled me and I felt myself jump in the sheets. "How long have you been awake?"

"The phone woke me," he said, sitting up and rubbing his back. "But this thing is not all that comfortable."

"Sorry," I mumbled.

"It's all good. But man, between last night and just now, that was the most ballsy I've ever heard you."

"Or stupid," I sighed.

I sat up in the bed, looked over at Katie, who was still asleep beside me, curled on her side, her arm crooked beneath her pillow. She looked peaceful, and as I stood up from the bed, I tried to be as quiet as possible.

"Either way, we better get that action figure or I'm completely screwed." I found my shoes on the ground and held them between my fingers as I spoke.

Dustin rolled off the hideaway and started pushing it back into the couch, replacing the cushions. He was not attempting to be near as quiet as me. "You're not in the wrong though. No one deserves to be tied to a thankless job when they're a teenager."

"Yeah but that job is my only chance to make some

money before I leave for college. I was depending on it to help pay my tuition."

"When we get that action figure, it won't even matter," he said.

I grabbed my backpack. "I'm going to hop in the shower. We should get on the road again soon." I looked to the alarm clock, the red LCD lights blaring bright in the dark. It was getting close to 9am.

"I'll get everyone awake," he said.

"Thanks." I stood up, grabbed my backpack and went into the bathroom. Despite Dustin's words of encouragement, I felt nauseous. I turned on the water and let the room fill with steam.

More than anything, I hoped he was right.

I *needed* him to be right.

"No way, dude," Dustin said with his mouth full, chewing on a muffin. "No way. Yoda having a lightsaber is completely contradictory to who he is in *Empire*. Remember *wars not make one great*? Yoda believed in the power of the Force over weapons."

"That's where you're wrong," Joel argued. "It's called *character development*. That's what Yoda learned from his failures. The Jedi were totally full of themselves, not knowing that the Sith were right under their noses. Yoda saw that weakness and used his time on Dagobah to *unlearn* what he'd learned. That's what he tells Luke."

I walked in on this conversation after getting out of the

bathroom and finding our hotel room empty. Since everyone's stuff was still on the ground, I assumed they'd all gone down to the lobby for the complimentary breakfast.

I was right; my friends sat at one of the breakfast tables that littered the dining area of the hotel's lobby. There were other people in here too, mostly families, parents with little kids. An older couple sat together, both of their faces hidden behind newspapers. There were two televisions on the walls, both of them tuned to the Weather Channel. My friends found a table near the back of the room, piles of fruit and muffins in front of them, bowls of cereal, at least a dozen pancakes. Katie was missing though.

"Hey!" Joel said as I sat down next to them. "Help me out here. Tell Dustin he's wrong about Yoda."

I pulled up a chair as Hannah scooted over to make space for me. She handed me a muffin and a plastic cup of orange juice. "Thank you," I said to her. "Where's Katie?"

"She went back up to the room to brush her teeth and get her stuff together. You must have just missed her."

"Bro," Dustin said, continuing the argument I walked into. "You only want him to agree with you because you know your argument doesn't hold weight by itself."

I smiled weakly, eating my muffin.

"What's wrong?" Hannah asked.

"Nothing," I said. "I just—"

"You look like you're going to be sick. Are you feeling alright?" Joel said. "Do you need a barf bag?"

"No, I don't need a barf bag." I sighed. "I quit my job."

"Whoa!" Joel said. "When?"

"Like twenty minutes ago?" I said. I drank the orange juice, trying to get some vitamins in my body.

"What?" Hannah said, her eyes wide.

"Yeah. Mr. Gilroy found out where we were. I called him last night and left a message on the machine at the store. He called our room this morning and told me I was selfish and undependable. So I quit."

"Holy shit," Joel said, leaning back in his chair. "Was that what the ringing was? The phone?"

"Yeah," I said. "I called from a payphone but I guess he tracked the number back to the hotel."

"Man, you can find anything on the internet," Dustin said.

"This is awful news. Where am I supposed to get my discounted ice cream now?" Joel feigned disappointment.

This made me crack a smile and I threw a crumb of blueberry muffin at him.

"I just really need this to work out," I said. "This whole trip. Because when we go back home, I'm unemployed. Whatever money I was hoping to make from working is up in smoke at this point."

Joel frowned.

"Maybe he was just angry in the moment," Hannah said. "Calling you selfish. Give him a few days to calm down and you can probably go and get your job back. I've seen the girls he has working there. None of them know as much as you do."

"I don't know," I said. "I was pretty rude to him on the

phone too. I guess I was still tired, and still angry at that Yoda guy and all this stuff just...boiled up."

"Hannah's right. It's going to be okay," Dustin said. "I mean, think about it. You're leaving for college in like eight weeks anyway. And even if you can't get your job back, this will give you a chance to just relax for the rest of the summer with a pocket full of money. This is a win in my opinion."

"Well, if I were to trust your opinion," I said, my smile cracking a little wider, "then I'd be wrong about Yoda too."

"I told you!" Joel almost yelled, shooting up out of his chair and pointing at Dustin.

Hannah and I both erupted in laughter.

CHAPTER 16

"It's okay," Dustin said. "Mr. Reynolds isn't scheduled to land in Houston until 10am tomorrow morning. All we have to do is get there before then."

"We're cutting it close. We were originally supposed to get the action figure today and head home," I said.

"Plus that means trying to find another place to sleep tonight," Hannah said.

The unfortunate thing was we were still seven hundred miles from our destination. No one would outright say it, but Dustin's mistake cost us valuable time and money—both of which were running thin.

"Look," he said, "I know it's not ideal, but as long as we get there first, we win. And we have time on our side," Dustin said.

I raised my eyebrows, unsure of his logic.

"Just think about it," he continued. "We know that Mr. Reynolds won't be there until well after ten because his flight doesn't even land until then."

"Are you sure?" Joel asked.

"Yes," he said. "I saw the tickets and everything on his desk. All we have to do is be there at the estate sale first thing tomorrow morning and buy it before he gets there. Easy peasy."

"Says the guy who told us the directions were easy," Katie almost whispered in my ear.

I gave her a knowing grin and then turned to the rest of the crew. "Well, if this is even going to work, we need to get on the road. We've got twelve hours of driving ahead of us," I said.

After everyone got a chance to shower and eat some of the free breakfast (as well as stuff our pockets with whatever food we could take) we left the hotel in St. Louis. I spent some time mapping out our way to Agloe. Katie even went down to the hotel's business center, which was a couple of desktop computer shoved in a corner, and wrote down the Mapquest directions on a pad of hotel paper.

I felt more confident now than I had the rest of the trip, mostly because I knew that Katie sat next to me as I drove. Taking the passenger seat, she had both the map and the handwritten directions in her lap, guiding me along the highways as we headed south toward Texas—and, hopefully, to our destination.

As I drove, I couldn't help but glance over at her a few times. Her hair was pulled back in a messy ponytail and any time she looked over at me, I could feel myself blush.

As my friends sat in the back, I could almost make myself believe that we were by ourselves.

She had her arm on the center console, and I imagined that if I put my arm there too, I could simply reach over and interlace our fingers. I found my imagination running rampant. If we were on a roadtrip together, where would we go? What would we do? If I were to reach over and lean my face close to hers, would she kiss me?

She must have caught me staring because she gave me a quizzical look. "You better pay attention to the road," she said playfully.

I blushed and turned my head to the passing stripes ahead of us. "Sorry."

"I'm just giving you a hard time," she said. I could tell she was looking at me as well, making me blush even harder.

"Do we, uh," I said, "want some music?"

"Yes!" Dustin said. "What do you guys want?"

I leaned over to Katie. "What do you want to listen to?"

She sat back in her seat. "Whatever you guys want. I'm going to take a nap."

"Okay," I said. Then, looking into the rearview mirror, I shrugged. "Whatever you want, Dustin."

"Nah," he said, dejected. "We should all probably just get some rest so one of us is ready to drive when you get tired."

Leaning against the door beside her, a sweater rolled up into a makeshift pillow, Hannah didn't even open her eyes to quip, "Well, let me be the first to tell you, Dustin—it won't be you."

Just after noon, we crossed into Arkansas and, judging by the gas gauge, knew we'd need to stop in the next town to fuel up. Katie leaned against the window of her door, fast asleep. In the backseat, both Hannah and Joel were asleep as well while Dustin read a comic book.

It was peaceful driving in silence, but also gave me a lot of time to think about my future and how much I was depending on this whole adventure to pan out, for things to go our way. Too many variables made it possible for us to fail, to lose out on this opportunity. It made me bite my thumbnail as I thought about it.

As I drove, Katie blinked awake and sat up, stretching.

"Where are we?" she asked quietly.

"Somewhere in Arkansas," I said. "Maybe a couple of hours from Little Rock?" We passed a road sign that said we were ten miles from Corning.

She pulled out her map and glanced at it. "Okay, we're about a hundred and fifty miles from Little Rock if we're in Corning. And," she said, smirking, "if we take the exit for Highway 64, we can be in Memphis by this evening."

"I heard that," Dustin said from the backseat. He had his headphones over his ears and a graphic novel in his hands.

"What are you reading?" Katie asked, turning in her seat.

"It's called *Dark Empire*," he said, showing her the cover. "It's about Luke Skywalker going to the Dark Side."

"Man," she said. "Sounds intense."

"It's pretty good," I said. "What's your favorite comic series?"

She turned back around to face me. "Well, I'm not really into like superheroes or corny stuff like that," she said. "Like, Superman wears his underwear on the outside of his suit? And people can't see that he's Clark Kent without glasses? I don't get it. So no superheroes. Well, except *Spawn*. My uncle gave me *Spawn* when I was in middle school. Oh, and *Sandman*. So, probably those two."

"*Sandman* is great," I said.

I first discovered Neil Gaiman's work when I was a sophomore in high school and it changed the way I approached graphic storytelling. I learned how to give characters depth through their words and their actions instead of just showing them looking strong through drawing them that way.

"You should read the book Josh is working on," Dustin said.

I gave him a panicked look through the rearview mirror. The last thing I wanted was for someone else to read what I'd been working on. Dustin and Joel had read it, but I trusted their input and knew they would appreciate how much I'd worked on it.

"I don't know," I started to protest.

"Oh come on," Dustin said. He leaned forward, pushing up in between the two seats. "Don't listen to him because he'd never admit it but it's really good. And if you're into *Sandman*, you'll like it."

Katie turned to me. "Well?"

"Well what?" I said, not taking my eyes off the road and feeling flush again.

"Come on. Let me read it."

I sighed, relenting. "Fine," I said. "It's in my backpack. It's not finished, you know."

"That's okay. Look, I didn't bring any reading material, and I'm bored out of my mind. I'd really like to read your comic," she said. "It's the space one, right? Indiana Jones in space?"

"Yeah," I said. "When we stop for gas, I'll pull it out of my backpack."

"Perfect," she said.

She may have just wanted to read something to abate her boredom, but my stomach was already in knots knowing that she would be reading my work.

CHAPTER 17

After stopping in the small Arkansas town just south of the Missouri border for gas, Joel offered to drive, and Hannah wanted the copilot's seat—promising both Katie and me that she would keep him on schedule and on the right path.

While I went in the gas station to pay for the fill-up, I found a payphone on the wall outside. With a couple of quarters in my pocket, I fed them into the slot and dialed my mom's office. After her assistant patched me through, I expected to hear my mom's voice on the other end, but it was someone else.

"What's up nerd?"

I sighed. It was my brother. "Jake, where's mom? And why aren't you you at work?"

"It's my lunch break, numbnuts. She ran some errands and to get us something to eat. Are you dorks lost? Do I need to call Greyhound?"

"No, we're not lost," I said through gritted teeth. "When will mom be back?"

"Where even are you?" He asked, ignoring my own question. That's how it was talking with Jake. It's like he couldn't even compute the words you were saying to him.

"Somewhere in Arkansas," I said. "Heading back home tomorrow."

"Arkansas? Mom said you were going to Texas."

"Arkansas is on the way, dumbass." I was losing my cool with him.

"How am I supposed to know that?"

"I swear you're just messing with me. Anyway, tell mom that we probably won't be back tomorrow like I originally told her. Most likely Saturday at this point."

"Your vehicle driving alright?"

I was taken aback by the question. "Uh," I stammered, "yeah."

"I mean, I'm sure you just got on the road without checking your oil levels or tire pressure or electrical connections," he said. "I'm surprised the engine hasn't exploded yet."

"It's *fine*," I said.

"You need to at least let me show you how to do some of that stuff," he said.

"Look Jake, I'm strapped for time. Just tell mom what I said."

"Yeah, let me see here," he said, drawing out his words. "Let me find a pen and paper. I didn't know I was going to play secretary..."

"Jake, stop being stupid and just tell mom, okay?" The payphone beeped at me, letting me know I was almost out of time. "Alright, I've got to go. Promise me you'll tell mom what I said."

"Sorry, I write slow," he said, talking over me. I could hear a pencil scratching on paper on the other end of the line. *"Ran into trouble. Got thrown in jail. Won't be back til Saturday."* He narrated this as he wrote.

"*Jake*," I said sharply. "Stop messing around." The payphone beeped again.

"Dude, lighten up. I've got it. I'll let her know—"

Then the line went silent. I hung the receiver back on its hook and let it hang there. Talking with him made me so frustrated sometimes. I felt like every time I needed him to take something seriously, he was unable to do it.

Back at the car, my friends were standing around, everyone awake and stretching their legs.

"Get me that comic," Katie said as I approached.

"Alright," I said. "But promise me you'll go easy on me."

"I won't lie to you if that's what you're saying. But your friends seem to think it's really good. And honestly, I'd even read Nathaniel Hawthorne right now."

"God," I said as I opened the back hatch and grabbed my backpack. "*The Scarlet Letter*? I think I'd rather get hit in the shin with a Razor scooter fifty times."

"I'd rather eat the rotten asshole of a roadkill skunk," she said.

"Wow," I said. "That was oddly, grossly specific."

"My sophomore English teacher made us read that and I hated every single page," Katie said. She leaned against the back fender as I scrounged around all of our belongings. "That bitch gave me an F on my paper too, and I've never forgiven her."

I found the book in my bag. It was spiral bound, filled with heavy art paper in which I'd hand-drawn panels on the blank sheets. For a second, I thought about shoving it back in the bag and telling her I didn't bring it or that I only brought my practice pad. Instead, I took a deep breath, pulled it out and handed it to her.

Katie took it and opened it to the first page.

"It's not done," I said as I shut the hatch. We crawled into the backseat, me taking the middle with her on one side and Dustin on the other.

"I don't mind."

"And it's just a first draft."

"Josh," she said, giving me a stern look. "It's okay." Katie held the book in her lap. "I think it's really cool to see the creative process. And when you make it big, I'll get to brag that I saw your original drawings."

While we were at the gas station, Dustin had found some batteries for his portable CD player and he fumbled with the device in his hands, shoving a disc in it from his collection. "If you guys don't mind," he said, "I'm going to try to get some rest now."

"Yeah, sure," I said.

He pulled the headphones over his ears and leaned

against the window, putting Hannah's rolled up sweater between his head and the glass.

Joel put the vehicle in drive and headed south, staying on the highway out of the small town. We'd grabbed some cheap snacks at the gas station and none of us felt like stopping for lunch or wasting anymore time than we needed to. Getting back on the road as quickly as possible was top priority, hoping we'd get to our destination in time to beat Mr. Reynolds to the purchase.

As Katie read, I couldn't help but lean over, see which page she was on, which panels caught her attention the most. See when and where she laughed; where she gasped, where she couldn't turn the page fast enough.

The book was technically four different issues in my mind, though only the first two were in color. The final issue was unfinished, some of the panels still only in pencil. It made me wish I'd had the whole thing done before she had her eyes on it. It made me self-conscious to share my work in progress with someone who I didn't really know.

"Hey," she said, looking up at me. "Get some shut eye. I'll let you know when I'm done."

"How is it? What do you think? Does it make sense?"

"I think you should get some rest."

"Ugh, fine," I said.

I leaned back as much as I could into the headrest behind me and shut my eyes, feeling the vibration of the road beneath us. My nervousness melted as the tires rumbled and I allowed myself to slip into a restless but much needed sleep.

I WOKE up and immediately knew something was wrong. The car was making a hum that didn't sound normal.

"Uh," Joel said from behind the steering wheel. He looked at me through the rearview mirror. "There's a problem with the acceleration. *There's no acceleration.*"

"What do you mean?" I asked. I felt the panic rise in me immediately, the fear rushing through my bloodstream.

"I mean I've got my foot all the way down on the pedal but nothing is happening. We're slowing down," he said.

I could feel the cars passing us as we pulled over to the side of the highway, the Jeep sputtering as it crawled forward.

"Where even are we?" I asked. "How long has this been happening?"

"It literally just started," Joel said. "I'm sorry, dude."

"It's not your fault," I said.

"This sucks. We're in the middle of nowhere," Dustin said.

"We're not in the middle of nowhere," Hannah said. "We're just outside of Little Rock."

"Oh my god," I said.

This was, aside from a wreck that totaled the car and injured either one or all of us, the worst-case scenario for this trip. We were already strapped for time, still so far from our destination and now we had a car that wouldn't accelerate.

There was an exit ramp just ahead of us. "Can you get us to that exit ramp?" I asked. "And get us off the highway?"

"I'm trying, man, but the steering wheel is really hard to turn. It's like all the electrical systems are shutting down." Joel banged the dash with the bottom of his fist. "Well," he said, "It worked for Han Solo."

"This unfortunately isn't the *Falcon*," I said.

"Your alternator is going out," Katie said.

"What?" I had no idea what that even was. As far as I knew, it could have been the flux capacitor or the hyperdrive and I would have been just as clueless.

"Your alternator. It's the thing attached to the motor that controls the electrical systems in the car," she said.

"I thought that's what the battery is for," I said. I knew I should have paid better attention in mechanic shop class my sophomore year, but I never was interested in cars the way my brother was.

"Oh my god," she said, clearly exasperated. "Do you guys not know anything? Your battery is what starts the car, gets it going. The alternator provides power, like a generator. Anyway, if your alternator goes out, it kills the battery and all your electrical goes dead."

The conversation I'd had with Jake echoed in my brain. He was right. I should have asked him to give the car a once-over before making the choice to take it on this roadtrip.

As Katie explained the situation, Joel was able to steer the dying vehicle off the highway and to the frontage road that ran parallel to it. There were a few businesses and houses out here, so we weren't exactly in the middle of nowhere, but, given the landscape, we were still nowhere near a payphone or even a mechanic.

The car sputtered to a stop and completely died. "Well," Dustin said. "Another happy landing."

"Not now," I said, unlocking the door and getting out. Usually I appreciated his ability to joke during serious situations, but right now I was feeling completely hopeless. I gestured to Joel, pointing to the latch beneath the steering wheel. "Can you pop the hood?"

Joel, looking despondent, did so. I unhooked the latch and propped the hood open with the metal bar that held it in place.

"Well?" Katie said as she appeared next to me. "What do you think?"

"I think," I said with a sigh, "that I have no idea what I'm looking at."

She pointed at a contraption on top of what I could only assume was the engine. It attached to some kind of cable that snaked its way across and over the different components. "That's the alternator," she said. "See that cable?" Katie traced a black line from the alternator. "It attaches to the battery. That's what gives the car its electrical power. But when it goes out, no power."

"How do you know all this?" I had never been more self-conscious, suddenly wishing I'd spent more time with my brother as he worked on his car. I never blamed my dad for what happened, but not having a father figure in my life who could teach me these things made me feel like I was missing some core knowledge set.

"I didn't want to take home ec my sophomore year and the only other option was mechanic shop," she said with a shrug.

"Well, I *did* take shop class, but now I regret not paying attention. So what do we do now?" I asked.

"We walk. We try to find a gas station nearby, see if they know of a local mechanic that can do it quickly."

"How long does it take to fix?" I asked. We were already way behind schedule and this just complicated things even further.

"A few hours," she said, shrugging her shoulders. "If they have the parts."

I sighed in exasperation. "We don't *have* a few hours. We're behind as it is."

As we talked, the rest of our friends piled out of the car. Dustin looked down the road. "Surely someone near by has a phone we can borrow."

"And call who?" I asked. "We don't know anyone who can help us. We're stuck in Arkansas with no car, no action figure and no plan!" I kicked the front bumper, and though it stung my toes, I didn't care. I welcomed the pain because it replaced the fear and anxiety. If I couldn't bite my thumbnail, this would be the next best option.

The thing was, the kick sounded like a bark. I kicked

again, and again it barked—until I realized it wasn't the bumper barking, but a dog.

From behind us, a shaggy brown dog stood near the edge of the road. His brown hair, wiry and thin, looked dirty. The dog had a black collar around his neck and wagged his tail and barked again. He cocked his head to the side and stared at the five of us.

Hannah knelt down on the asphalt and called him over. Slowly, as if he didn't quite trust us, the dog walked over and licked Hannah's outstretched hand.

"Are you lost, buddy?" she asked.

The dog rolled over on his back, his feet pawing at the air, begging to be scratched and rubbed.

"Let him go," Dustin said. "We have more important things to worry about right now."

"Maybe he belongs to someone near by," she said, looking up the road.

"Maybe he got out from someone's fence," Joel said. He knelt next to Hannah and scratched the dog's ear.

"Does he have a tag on his collar?" Katie asked.

"Yeah, but he won't sit still." As Hannah tried to check the name tag on the collar, the dog rolled back over on his feet and ran circles around her.

Finally, Hannah was able to get the collar situated and read the small metal name tag attached.

"Holy shit," she said. She turned to us, huddled next to the dead Cherokee, and smiled.

"What?" Joel asked.

"His name," she said, "is Chewbarka."

CHAPTER 18

We all huddled around the dog and he continued to wag his tail, letting us pet his belly and rub his ears.

"Where do you live?" Hannah asked him. She looked up and down the road, looking for a house or some other building where he might have come from.

"Should we walk up there, ask somebody if he belongs to them?" Joel asked.

Ahead of us on the frontage road, no more than a half a mile, a gas station sign was shining high in the clear blue sky.

"At the very least, we can find a payphone," Hannah said. "And hopefully call a mechanic."

"Or a Greyhound bus," I said.

Everyone looked at me, dumbfounded.

"What?" I said. "Look at us! We're stranded in the middle of nowhere, six hundred miles from home. We still have seven hours to drive and—newsflash—we're broken down on the side of the highway. Guys, we failed. This has been fun but we're out of time, out of money and out of a car."

"We still have plenty of money," Hannah started to argue.

"Not if we have to pay to replace whatever is broken here," I said. "Look, let's be realistic. We have to wait to get the car fixed, and even if it took just two hours, we still have almost seven hours to drive to Agloe. Mr. Reynolds will *for sure* be there in the morning. We're cutting it close as it is."

My friends all stood around me on the side of the road as I went on this tirade. In my defense, nothing had gone right this entire trip. What was supposed to be a quick there-and-back had suddenly ballooned into more than any of us had anticipated. The broken down vehicle was just the icing on the shit luck cake.

"We still have eighteen hours between now and when Mr. Reynolds lands in Houston," Dustin said. He came up beside me, calm and collected, though I could see right through the charade. The only thing he was trying to do was keep everyone else from also freaking out. "We can get the vehicle fixed and get back on the road. We can take turns driving, even if it takes all night. We can still do this."

"Dustin," I said, fuming, "this is real life, okay? This is not some roadtrip buddy movie. We are stuck, we are broke and we are done. We walk up to that gas station, we find a payphone and we get a bus home." I turned to

Hannah, still clutching the dog. "And we leave that mutt here."

"Hey!" Hannah said, holding the dog closer to her chest.

Katie sidled up next to me. "Come on," she said, putting a hand on my arm. The gesture was calming, as was her voice. "Let's start walking."

I didn't say another word, just turned to walk toward the gas station when a truck rumbled up behind us. I instinctively moved closer to the edge of the road, where the asphalt met grass, but the truck never passed us.

Then, a voice, male and gruff, called out, "Chewie? Is that my Chewie?"

We all turned and the dog leapt out of Hannah's grasp, landed on the pavement and bolted for the truck.

A man hopped out of the idling vehicle and knelt to the ground, scooping the dog up in his arms, letting it lick him all over his face. The man was middle-aged and but muscular and his greying hair was a stark contrast to his dark skin. He had a goatee that was almost as white as the hair on his head and a pair of blue canvas coveralls that looked stained with motor oil.

"Good boy," the man said. "But don't you ever run off again." Then he looked up at us. "Thank you for taking care of him, keeping him out of the road. These trucks drive by through here too fast. They'd squash him like a pup pancake without hesitation."

"You're welcome," Hannah said. "We were just going

to walk up to the gas station and call the number on his tag."

"Well I'm glad I found you all. He ran off from the yard when I was doing some work, chased off some rabbit or something I'm sure. I've been looking for him for damn near an hour," he said. Chewie the dog had settled down as the man cradled him. Then, the man saw the dead vehicle and the realization of what was going on struck him. "You kids stranded?"

"Yeah," I said. "Our car broke down."

"The alternator is dead," Katie said.

"Oh damn," he said, raising his eyebrows. "Well hell, let me tow you guys back to my shop and we can have a look at it."

"Are you sure?" I said. "We don't want to impose. We're just going to walk to the gas station and make a phone call."

"Not imposing at all. Where are you kids from?" The man placed the dog in the driver's seat of his truck.

"Indianapolis," Dustin said. "We're on our way to Texas."

"You all are a long way from home then," he said with a whistle. "And sounds like you got a long way left to go." He walked toward us. "My shop is just a mile and a half up the road. Let me tow you all back and see if we can get you back on your journey." He then extended his hand. "I'm a mechanic. My name's Lando."

. . .

Lando hooked the Jeep to the back of his truck with a couple of tow cables and pulled us to his shop, a metal building off the highway. A sign, rusted and worn, was hung above the door. It read *Lando's Auto and Body*.

The shop was full of auto parts and half-built cars and a small office was carved out on one side of the shell, enclosed in sheetrock. It was messy, paper invoices all over the metal desk, a filing cabinet and a couple of chairs set up. Hannah and Katie sat on the chairs while the three of us guys sat on the dusty floor as we waited for some word from Lando. Chewbarka stayed in the office with us and we all took turns playing with him and rubbing his belly, which he seemed to enjoy quite a bit.

"I can't believe we found a dog named Chewie," Hannah said as the dog rolled in her lap.

"And he lives with Lando," Joel said.

"It's fate," Dustin said. "Our luck hasn't run out. We've got Lando on our side."

"It's just a coincidence," I said. "We just happened to be in this town when we broke down."

Katie gave me a look, her eyes narrowed, and I kept my mouth shut for the rest of the time that we sat there, waiting for Lando to work on the Jeep. I kept thinking about how much this would cost, how much money we had left and if we'd even be able to pay for the repair with what we had. I couldn't afford to dip anymore into my college savings—though it may all be for nothing anyway.

"Hey," Katie said, nudging me with her shoulder. She had come to sit down beside me on the concrete floor and we leaned against the wall. All I wanted was to go back home and worry about how I was going to pay for art school without this elaborate scheme that seemed to go wrong every step of the way.

I raised my eyebrows without answering her.

"Lighten up a little, okay? We'll be alright."

I just grunted and she left me alone, turning her attention to the dog, who welcomed it.

After an hour or so of waiting, Lando came into the office from the door that led to the shop.

"Well, I've got good news and bad news," he said. "It's definitely the alternator, and I can definitely fix it and get you kids back on the road."

"What's the bad news?" I asked.

"I can't get a new one in until tomorrow."

CHAPTER 19

I STOOD AT THE EDGE OF THE DIRT ROAD THAT CUT THE path from the highway to Lando's shop. I felt like I was going to cry. We were stuck. The only thing I could think to do was to call my mom or Jake, have one of them drive the nearly six hundred miles to come pick us up.

Though, even if they did, Lando could have the Cherokee done by then anyway. Either way, there was no way we were getting to Agloe tonight or even in the morning.

I heard footsteps from behind me, shuffling in the dirt and I already knew who it was.

"Don't," I said as Dustin appeared beside me.

"Come on, man," he said. "We're so close. There's a chance that—"

"That what?" I asked. "That we miraculously get to Agloe before your boss? That the action figure is still there by the time we get there? It's not going to happen, Dustin."

I could feel the anger rising in my voice and in my body, the heat crawling up the back of my neck.

"Maybe there's another option," he said.

"There's not and we're stuck. We're *stuck*, okay? Every decision you've made on this trip has got us nowhere."

"Come on, man," he said. "That's not fair."

"It's completely fair. You were the one who talked us into this. You were the one who left the map. You were the one who got us lost and off course."

"And you were the one who rescued us," he said. "You were the one who got us that hotel in St. Louis. You were able to win that tournament. You can't give up on this now. Not when we're so close."

"It's too late, man. I'm sorry. We just have to call it."

"I'm not giving up," Dustin said. "I'm not going to tell our friends that we came all this way for nothing just for a little setback."

"A little setback? Newsflash, idiot, we have no car!" I screamed the last words, almost in his face. My own rage caught me off guard, but it had been building in me, boiling until spewing out uncontrolled.

Dustin took a step back and just stared at me. I just crossed my arms defiantly, refusing to feel ashamed for my sudden explosion of anger.

"Dude," he said. "You need to get ahold of yourself."

Turning, he walked back to the shop. Our friends were huddled by the front door, watching this whole interaction, and embarrassment washed over me. I didn't know what to do, so I just started walking, going up the dirt path and to the highway. I turned onto the asphalt and let my feet take over, my mind completely empty.

I DIDN'T KNOW how long I'd been walking, but I eventually came to a convenience store that looked like its better years had long passed. Still, walking inside, I welcomed the air conditioning after being in the Arkansas summer heat. I could feel that my face was sunburned, my cheeks stinging.

I replayed the argument with Dustin in my head over and over. Sure, we'd had disagreements over the years, but never had we come to full-on screaming fits.

Well, *he* hadn't.

Maybe I was the problem. Maybe I was the one holding them back. I chewed at my thumbnail, grabbing a corner of it with my front teeth and gnawing at it until it came loose. The skin stung where the thumbnail had come off and I closed my fist around it. The pain in my thumb masked the retreating anger in my mind.

"Something I can help you find?" the cashier was an older woman with skin that looked like leather, creases and lines etched over decades of living.

"No, I'm just..." I trailed off. *Just what*? I asked myself. *Just escaping from my friends? Just hiding from our failure?*

I fished in my pockets for change, but didn't have any quarters. I decided I would just call my mom and tell her what was going on and see if either she or my brother could come get us. I would figure out what to do with my car later.

Approaching the counter, I pulled out a dollar. "Can I have some quarters?" I asked. "I need to use the payphone."

"I'm sorry, son," the woman said. "Payphone ain't been workin' lately. Got someone from Bell supposed to come fix it."

I sighed. *Of course.*

"Nevermind." I would have to figure out something else. From the walk, my mouth was parched, so I explored the soda options.

At the back of the store, I opened one of the coolers and pulled a Mountain Dew. It made me feel selfish, buying a drink for myself and not my friends. After a moment's hesitation, I filled my hands, stacking six bottles total—one even for Lando—and took them to the front counter. I produced the money from my pocket and carried the sodas out in a plastic sack. I was prepared to walk all the way back to Lando's place when a familiar truck pulled into the parking lot, the engine rumbling as it idled to a stop.

Katie stepped out of the passenger seat.

"How did you know where I was?" I asked.

"I didn't," Katie said. She gestured back to Lando, who sat in the driver's seat of the idling truck. Chewbarka popped his head out of the open window of the passenger door and barked at us. "I asked him where the closest payphone was."

I gave out a small chuckle. "Well, it's broken."

"That's good. For me."

I immediately felt guilty for thinking about bailing on my friends so I held up the plastic sack in my grip meekly. "I bought us all Mountain Dew."

"That's sweet of you. I could go for some caffeine."

I pulled out two of the bottles and handed one of them to Katie, who twisted the cap and took a long drink. "You nerds have good taste in soda."

I laughed. "Thanks." I opened mine as well.

Katie sat on the concrete curb in front of the store and I joined her.

"Sorry about being a jerk back there," I said. "I am just...lost, I guess. Both figuratively and literally. We are six hundred miles from home and I don't know how we're going to get back."

"I understand," she said. "But I'm not who you should be apologizing to."

I hung my head in shame. "Yeah."

"I get it though."

"It's not just this," I said. "I mean, I quit my job for this. I am still at least eighteen thousand dollars away from paying my tuition and I have less than two months to get it paid. I guess I was depending on this to work out, more than I would even admit to myself."

"That's why we need to keep going. We owe it to each other see this to the end, even if it doesn't end the way we hope."

"Still, that means that I'll be going back home with no job, no money and no plan for my tuition."

"It's not the end of the world, though, right?" Katie asked. She took another drink. "I mean, yeah, it's not ideal. But there are other jobs. And is there a hard and fast rule that you *have* to go to college right after graduation?"

I didn't answer. My biggest fear was not getting into art school. My second biggest fear was being stuck in Greenwood with the opportunity right in front of me, but unable to take it.

"I read your book," she said. "The whole thing. While you were asleep."

"Yeah?" I asked. It felt like a waste of time now. I had spent so much energy and so many hours working on that book, hoping that it would prove that I was an artist worthy of being at the Art Institute. Instead, it was just a *thing*. It was nothing more than fan fiction.

"It's *really* good, and I'm not just saying that. You are an amazing artist, and you should be proud of yourself. Don't count yourself short, Josh."

"What am I supposed to do now though?" I said. "Even if I can draw, even if the book is good, what am I supposed to do with it? I can't get the attention of the publishers without getting into art school. I can't get into art school without the money, and I can't get the money because every part of this trip has been a goddamn failure."

"Not every part," she said, staring at me. In that moment, I realized how close Katie was sitting to me, how

I could smell the lip balm on her lips. It made me blush and I looked away.

She was right. We owed it to each other to keep going, to find a way until we had no other option. And I wanted to be close to her like this for as long as I could.

"Hey you kids," Lando called out from the truck. "You good?"

I stood up from the curb and held out my hand. "Come on," I said. Katie took it and I lifted her from the ground. "Let's go back and see what we can do from here."

CHAPTER 20

Lando drove, Chewbarka in his lap, the truck bouncing with every dip and pothole in the dilapidated road that led back to his shop. The radio was turned low, an old rock and roll song playing on the speakers, cutting in and out with static.

We told him all the aspects of our plan, of why we were driving from Indiana to Texas, and he chewed on his lip as if he were trying to compute it all.

"So you're telling me," he said, "that you kids are driving across the country for some toy?"

"Not just any toy," I said. "It's a prototype that's worth a ton of money. Well, according to Dustin."

"I didn't believe it at first," Katie said. She sat in the middle of the bench seat, and Chewbarka made his way over to settle in her lap. She stroked his wiry hair and he licked at her hand. "But it's true. All of it. This action figure is worth a lot. I wouldn't have come if it wasn't real."

"It's funny. When I was a kid, I loved *Star Wars*. And

even though we were poor, and didn't have much money, I saw it probably six times at the theatre. After that, every stick I found was a lightsaber. And then when the second movie came out, there was this character that not only looked like me, but we had the same name," Lando said. "That changed my life. There was this guy, in this movie that I loved, that I could literally see myself in. After that, I was hooked, you know? I read everything I could find. Read comic books. Drew pictures. Collected the toys."

He looked down at the dog, gave him a loving scratch on the chin. The dog closed his eyes and lifted his head to the touch. "Found my own Chewie. So I get it. You do funny things for the things you love. The characters and the stories, they're not just movies. They're real, they live in your heart and in your imagination."

That was exactly how I felt. That's why I started drawing, why I wanted to write my own comic books. Because those characters and those stories opened up my imagination.

"I get it, I do," I said. "But I guess we had our hopes up on this trip. I mean, what did we think? We were going to drive across the country and nothing would go wrong? That we'd find this action figure and get it and be rich?"

"Isn't that what *Star Wars* is all about though?" Lando said, glancing at me. "Isn't it about hope? Hell, that first movie, they started calling it *A New Hope* after it came out."

"Hope only gets you so far," I said with a sigh.

"No, son," Lando said. He glanced over at me. "Hope

is what gets you the rest of the way when you can't go any further on your own."

"Well," I said. "What are we supposed to do now? We can't get back on the road until you get the alternator fixed. And the estate sale is tomorrow. Even if we left first thing in the morning, the action figure would be gone by the time we get to Texas."

"I have an idea," Lando said. "And it might be just as crazy as driving a thousand miles for a toy."

I looked to Katie who just shrugged her shoulders. But something in her eyes told me that she already knew what Lando had in mind.

We stood outside Lando's shop, huddled around, drinking Mountain Dew. My friends were thankful for the cold drinks.

I gestured to Dustin and pulled him away from the group. "I'm sorry," I said to him. "I'm sorry for yelling at you and for calling you an idiot. I was just so frustrated. I felt like nothing has been going right on this trip."

"Don't worry about it. To be fair, if we'd brought my car, I'd be just as upset. I should be more realistic."

"If we brought your car," I said, "we wouldn't have made it out of Indiana. *That* is realistic."

He laughed. "Yeah, you're probably right."

"No," I said. "In all reality, I should do better at seeing the bright side of things."

Lando had disappeared into his work area and came

back outside. He found Dustin and me and coughed into his hand, getting our attention. "Grab the rest of your friends," he said. "And then you kids follow me."

Through the large overhead door, we walked into the shop, winding our way through half-built cars and other parts. My Jeep was sitting in the middle, the hood open, a cart of tools beside it. The bad alternator had been taken out and Lando had it sitting on the cart as well, just waiting to replace it with the new unit.

"So here's the deal. You kids need to get to Texas before tomorrow, but your car is broken down," he said. "And because we won't get the parts til tomorrow, we need to find an alternative so y'all can get back on the road." He stopped beside a a large canvas cover, with something hidden beneath it. "I think I have a solution."

He pulled the canvas off and my mind went blank. Beneath it was a car, an old one. It was silver and looked like a classic, at least thirty years old, with a hood as long as my Cherokee. The door handles, despite sitting under the dusty covering, were chrome and shining, reflecting the light of the overhead lamps.

"What are you saying?" I asked, though I knew what he was telling us, what his solution was.

"You kids need to get to Texas tonight, and you can't do it in your car. So you can take this one," Lando said.

"What is it?" Joel asked.

"This," Lando said, "is a 1977 Ford Falcon."

A *Falcon*. It was only fitting.

Lando continued, "You go down to Texas, do what you

got to do, and by the time you come back through here tomorrow, I'll have your car fixed up and ready to go. You'll be able to get back home with a running Jeep."

I gulped. "You know we can't pay you," I said. "We don't have much money as it is."

"I never said anything about payment," Lando said. "All you got to do is come back in one piece. I'll take care of the rest."

"I can't believe it," I said as I approached the vehicle. It was immaculate and clean, the silver paint reflective in the light of the shop.

"It may not look like much, but she's got it where it counts," Lando said with a wink.

"It's perfect," I said.

My friends joined me, looking in the windows and gawking over the vehicle.

"Go ahead and fire it up," Lando insisted. He held the keys out to me and I took them, almost reverently.

Opening the door, I settled in the driver's seat and turned the ignition. The car rumbled to life and eased into a steady purr.

"You kids better get on the road if you're to get to Texas tonight," Lando said.

Twenty minutes later, we had our bags, belongings and everything transferred from the cargo hold of the Jeep and packed into the car's trunk.

As we prepared to leave, Lando held out his hand for a handshake but we all hugged him instead.

"How can we ever repay you?" I asked him.

"Look kid, the Force may not be real, but *Star Wars* showed me that the goodness of people is. You look for ways to help the people around you, and it'll come back to you. I've always believed that." He gave me a slight smile. "Always had hope in it."

"Thank you," I said, choking up.

"You're welcome. See you kids tomorrow."

"See you tomorrow," I repeated.

I got in the driver's seat, with Katie taking shotgun. She had the map folded in her lap, ready to give us directions and navigate us to Agloe.

"Ready?" I asked everyone.

Joel and Dustin, with Hannah between them, all beamed from the backseat. I put the car in drive and we headed south, toward Texas. With luck—or hope or the Force—on our side, we would be in Agloe before midnight.

We pulled out onto the highway and I reached for the radio.

"How about some music?" I asked.

"Does this thing even have a CD player?" Dustin asked. He already had his binder in his lap, ready to find us something to listen to.

The Falcon, however, didn't have a CD player, just a cassette deck. There was already a tape loaded so I ejected what was in it and took a look. I couldn't help but smile ear to ear.

It was Bon Jovi.

I put the cassette back in, turned the volume knob and let the music play.

CHAPTER 21

The Falcon rode like a dream on the highway and anytime I had to accelerate to pass another car, it roared with power. When the sun went down and the warm weather waned to an early summer cool, we lowered the windows. Katie held her hand out the passenger side and moved her fingers in the wind like she was playing the piano. The wind blowing through the car whipped her hair and it shimmered in the light of the setting sun.

I couldn't help but stare, be smitten, completely enamored. She was gorgeous and alive with happiness and I wanted to share every moment of it.

We stopped for gas in Nacogdoches, a town in far east Texas, the trees tall and enveloping the highway that led to Agloe. As we approached the Houston area, and Agloe to the far east side of the city, we could see the glow of it in the distance. I was already getting antsy, my knee bouncing with anticipation, my palms slick with sweat.

We'd made it.

After everything that had gone wrong, we finally pulled into the Agloe city limits just after ten that night.

Dustin, sleeping in the backseat, sat up, rubbing his eyes. “Are we...?” he asked.

“Yeah,” I said.

Agloe, though just on the outskirts of Houston, felt a lot like Greenwood and its proximity to Indianapolis. I could smell the salty air out of the windows and I pulled into a gas station’s parking lot and sidled up next to a pump. The parking lot was large and brightly lit.

I turned off the ignition and we all piled out of the car, stretching our legs.

Dustin and Joel were both beaming and they came over to me, almost barreling me over in a bearhug.

“We did it!” Dustin exclaimed. “We made it!”

“Now we just have to find where we’re going to sleep tonight,” Joel said. “No chance you can swindle someone to pay for us a hotel again is there?”

“First, I didn’t swindle anyone. We almost lost our car to that lunatic.” I couldn’t believe that had been only twenty-four hours previous, when we’d been lost in St. Louis and I found myself playing in an illegal Star Wars card game with our vehicle on the line.

Now here we were, in our destination, in a different car, but here nonetheless.

“I’m going to fill up the car, and we can figure out what to do from here. We still have to find exactly where this estate sale is going to be in the morning,” I said.

“Oh shit,” Joel said. “I didn’t even think about that.”

The directions to the address were on the original Mapquest pages that he'd printed off and lost, but I already had a plan for finding it in the morning.

"It's okay," I said. "I've got it under control."

Both of them looked at me like I was a stranger they'd never met. "How exactly do you have it under control?" Joel asked.

"We'll use the Force," I said with shrug.

He narrowed his eyes. "That's not how the Force works," he said.

"Don't worry. Let's just take it easy tonight."

"Hey guys," Hannah called out. "Katie and I are going inside."

"Hang on a second," I said. I took my wad of cash out of my pocket and handed Katie forty dollars. "Tell them we need this on pump six."

She nodded.

"Thanks," I said. "I'm going to fill up and make a phone call."

Dustin and Joel followed the girls in while I pumped the gas. Once the tank was full, not quite forty dollars, I went in to get my change and find a payphone.

While my friends filled their hands with snacks and drinks—we hadn't eaten since early this afternoon, when we left Lando's place—I found the payphone, fed it a couple of quarters and dialed our house number.

After a couple of rings, my mom answered, her voice tired and groggy.

"Josh?" she asked.

"Hey mom. Sorry it's late."

"God, I was hoping it was you," she said. "I've been worried sick. I got your message from your brother, but I didn't know if you'd call again. Where are you?"

"I know, I'm sorry. I just wanted to call and let you know that we've made it. We made it to Agloe."

"Wow," she said. "That's great. Listen, I wanted to let you know that you got another letter from the art institute today."

My heart dropped. I could tell from her tone it wasn't good news. "Yeah?"

"It says that if your tuition isn't paid in full by the first of August, they're going to rescind your application. I'm so sorry. You know if I could, I'd write them a check right now."

"Don't worry about it, mom," I said. "That's what this is about. This whole trip. I'm going to take care of it."

I could tell that she was sobbing.

"Don't cry, mom. Seriously. You have done more for me than I could ever thank you for, but this is something that I am going to take care of," I said. "I have to do this myself."

"Your dad would be so proud of you," she said. "I hope you know that."

I could feel the tears welling up in the corners of my eyes as well.

"I do," I finally said. "I'll see you Saturday."

"Okay," she said. "Please be safe."

"We have been."

The phone made a noise, signaling that our time was almost up. "I've got to go, mom. I love you."

"I love you," she repeated.

The line went silent and I hung up the receiver.

"Everything alright?"

I turned to see Katie behind me. I swiped my eyes with the sleeve of my shirt. "Yeah," I said. "Yeah, I'm good. Just called my mom, let her know that we made it."

"And you're sad about that?"

I couldn't help but laugh, which helped push the tears away. "No. It's something else. But I promise, everything is alright." I nodded to the convenience store. It was huge, much bigger than the place we'd spent time at outside of Little Rock, the place where she and I had sat on the curb and drank Mountain Dew.

"If you say so."

"Did you get more cigarettes?" I asked.

She hesitated. "No," she finally said.

I raised my eyebrows.

"I'm quitting."

"That's a shame. Just when I was getting started, too."

She gave me a look. "Okay, smartass. Look, I just have done a lot of thinking on this trip, and what I want for myself. The habits I'd picked up in high school. And I don't want to do it anymore. Besides, it could be worse. At least my thumbnails are intact." With that, she gave me a sarcastic smile.

I returned it with a sardonic look of my own and didn't

ask any further questions. The rest of our friends came out of the convenience store.

"Well?" Dustin said. "What do we do now?"

"I feel like we should find some place to spend the night," Hannah said. "But that probably means sleeping in the car."

I knew that option didn't really sound very appealing to any of us, but at this point, I didn't think we had any other option.

I was so nervous now anyway, I didn't know how much sleep I would be getting. I was simultaneously amped up and exhausted. It was this dichotomy of feeling that had me unable to really make a decision in this moment.

"Surely there's something else we can do," Joel said. "The Falcon is nice, don't get me wrong, but I feel like trying to sleep in that car would be awful."

"Yeah," Dustin said.

"Hey," Katie said. "We all brought our own blankets, right?"

Everyone looked to her. We had packed sleeping bags, thinking that we would have to sleep either in the Jeep or somewhere outside on this trip, if we stopped to sleep at all. According to the original idea for this trip, we were only expecting to spend the one night in Memphis. None of us had planned on the things that would go wrong–for better or worse.

"What do you have in mind?" I asked.

"I was just thinking," she said. "When I was looking at

the map, I noticed that we're only about an hour's drive from the beach. It would be a shame to drive all this way, be this close to the ocean and not see it."

We all nodded in understanding.

"I like it," I said. It sounded like the best idea that we could possibly have in that moment, much better than all of us cramped in the car and trying to get some rest in it. "Let's go to the beach."

CHAPTER 22

We piled back in the Falcon and Katie gave me directions to Galveston Island, a beach south of Agloe. The route took us on the outskirts of Houston and we could see downtown cutting into the darkness, the lights of the city bright against the stars of the night sky.

"Houston, Texas," Joel said, pointing to the lights in the distance. "You'll never find a more wretched hive of scum and villainy." Then he laughed. "Sorry, I have always wanted to say that."

"Guys," Dustin said, staring out the window, "I didn't think we'd be going to a beach. I didn't bring swim trunks."

"Dustin," Katie said, rolling her eyes. "None of us did. Remember, you had us getting here in one night. It'll be alright though."

"When I was a little kid, probably in the third grade, my dad took my brother and me to one of the Great Lakes," Hannah said. "We spent the night fishing and hanging around the campfire. Even to this day, that was one of my favorite trips growing up. It seemed so simple, you know? Do you think we'll be able to have a fire?"

"My grandparents had a place in Myrtle Beach," Joel said. "We spent every summer there, up until my Nana died. That was right before seventh grade. We haven't been back since."

I brought my thumbnail to my lips and glanced at Katie. Instead, I returned my hand to the steering wheel and gripped it tight. If she could leave her bad habits behind, so could I.

She reached for the stereo controls and turned the knob until she found a station that she liked. It was pop music and we kept the windows down as we drove on the highway to Galveston. It took a little over an hour to drive to the beach and we crossed a large bridge that spanned over some sort of bay between the mainland and the island. The water was deep blue but small waves would reflect the light from above, creating tiny sparkles that would appear at random, making it look like glitter in the darkness.

Once on the island itself, Katie navigated us to a public beach parking area. I pulled into the lot, putting five dollars in the overnight parking meter. The lot wasn't nearly full, but a few cars there told us the beach wouldn't be completely empty either.

We gathered our belongings from the car, the sleeping bags and our backpacks, and trekked from the parking lot across a two-lane road that separated the lot from the beach access. The stars burned brightly above us and the sounds of the waves lightly crashing against the sand was steady and soothing. My eyes had adjusted enough to the low light to see the path that we walked on, these sand-covered planks that gave way to the sand and the beach.

"Wow," Hannah said as we came over the crest of a sand dune that opened up to the entire beachhead. For as far as we could see in either direction in the low light of the full moon and the stars, the beach stretched out in front of the gulf waters. The waves were light and the surf low. There was only a slight breeze that blew in from the south and it felt perfect.

"This is amazing," Joel said as he pulled her close. "Great idea, Katie."

"Yeah," I said, close to her. "This is awesome."

"I was hoping it would be," she said.

We walked down a little further closer to the water until we found a spot that was level and the sand wasn't wet. Placing our sleeping bags on the ground, we all sat down for a moment, taking in the water and the beach.

"Should we find some wood?" Dustin asked. "We should have bought some stuff to make hot dogs and s'mores."

"Yeah," I said. My stomach growled, and we hadn't had a proper meal in almost twelve hours. Hot dogs cooked over an open flame sounded amazing, but for now we would have to settle for peanut butter sandwiches and whatever other snacks we had on hand. "A fire sounds great."

Thirty minutes later, after gathering enough wood to

start a decent fire, we dug a pit in the sand and sat around it as the flames slowly licked the air. The smoke billowed softly, and the fire illuminated our faces.

We ate our sandwiches, washing them down with already lukewarm sodas. Still, it was the best thing I'd ever eaten, the company making the meal taste better than it had any business being.

There was a sense of peace over all of us, I could feel it, almost like a religious experience. We ate, we laughed, we talked about the trip.

"Indianapolis Comic Con is at the end of the month," Dustin said. "That would be a great way to announce our new comic shop."

"And," Joel said, "a great place to find a buyer for the Boba Fett."

"That's what I was thinking," Dustin said. "Even if we don't sell it outright there, I know we'll make the connections to list it in an auction. That's what Mr. Reynolds does with his expensive collectibles."

"However we do it," I said, "I have to make my tuition payment by the first of August."

"No worries," Dustin said. "We've got this in the bag."

I wish I shared his optimism, but it was hard not to in this moment. Right now, everything was going our way, everything felt like the universe was on our side.

It had to be. Our futures depended on all this, and I felt like, at this moment, with my friends around me, that we'd *earned* it. We didn't just find a high-dollar collectible, it wasn't just another piece of our portfolio. This was it, this was our future on the line. It should have filled me with anxiety, but Dustin's optimism, the smiles of my friends, the cool wind in my hair made me feel like all of this was not only possible but fully in our grasp.

Joel turned to Katie, taking a bite of his sandwich. "You still haven't told us what you're going to do with your share of the money."

"That's because I still don't know what I'm going to do with it, to be honest," she said. "I've never had money in my life, no more than a few twenties after a birthday, you know?"

"If I didn't have to pay my tuition, I feel like I would be the same way," I said.

"I think more than anything, I would want to just have it to be comfortable," she said. "My mom has been a single mom for almost as long as I can remember at this point so we've never had a lot of money, you know?"

Hannah gave her a look that said that she understood. They were cousins after all.

Katie continued, "So just to be comfortable, to not have to worry about it myself, to know that if something were to happen, I would have this nest egg, it would take a weight off my shoulders."

"That's why I want to use it to find our own place," Hannah said. "Get out from under my mom and stepdad's roof."

"Well," Dustin said, "I'll make sure that our comic book shop will keep a roof over all our heads. We're going to have the best shop on the planet."

Hannah already was rolling her eyes because we all—save, perhaps Katie—had heard this so-called plan at least a dozen times.

"Don't roll your eyes," he said. "You know what I'm talking about. We won't charge table fees. We'll be a fun, safe place for anyone to come hang out, to come play and to come buy comic books. And of course we'll have the latest Josh McCreary right up front. Autographed copies and everything."

"If we don't charge table fees," Hannah said, "how will we make money?"

Table fees at a comic book shop like Galaxy were charged to rent a table for a specific amount of time for either tabletop or RPG games. None of us liked it, but it was only logical.

"I've already thought this through," Dustin said. "We stock plenty of snacks and sell them at a high enough markup to make up for it."

"That's..." Hannah said, "not a bad idea actually. I like it. By enticing them to stay longer, they buy snacks, drinks, things like that to make up for the lack of table fees." She turned to Joel. "What do you think?"

"I think it just might work." Joel leaned into Hannah and kissed her on the forehead. It was a sweet gesture, one that I had seen him do a thousand times over the last few years that they had been a couple. It was also one that, in this specific moment, I wished I could replicate with Katie.

CHAPTER 23

"Hey," Katie said as she walked up and sat next to me on the sand.

The fire had died down, and I had no idea what time it was, but I did know that the rest of our friends were sound asleep, having spread their sleeping bags out on the sand.

I had got up from mine and slowly walked down to the shoreline, sitting in the damp sand, letting the water lick my toes as it ebbed back and forth. I watched the stars on the horizon twist, the lights from boats twinkle and disappear.

"Hey," I repeated.

"Can't sleep?" she said.

"Not really."

"Whatcha thinking about?"

"My dad," I said.

My friends, talking about what all they would do with their share of the money, the things they wished for, made me think of him. There were so many questions I never got to ask him. Like, what *would* he do with a twenty thousand dollar windfall? What kinds of things would he wish for or what did he daydream about? Would he spend it on a family vacation? Would he buy my mom a new vehicle? All of these things that I wondered about him. I knew what kind of dad he was, but what kind of dreams did he have? What kind of wishes?

"Hannah told me," she said.

"I mean," I said, "it was a long time ago. And what did she say? *Hey, I think you'd like my friend Josh, but his dad is dead*?"

"Wow," she said, "that's exactly what she said, how did you know?"

She nudged me with her shoulder and I did it back. This playful little gesture felt flirtatious in a way, and I welcomed it. Over the last two days, we'd spent so much time together. She'd seen me at my most confident and at my lowest. Yet she still found a way to make me feel welcome in my own skin, welcome to just be me.

"I was eight," I finally said. "It was one of those freak accident things, you know?" I stared out at the water. "He was working in the attic, running some cabling for the television. He had bought this huge tv, right? One of those big fifty inch rear projection models, and there wasn't a cable hookup in the living room where my mom wanted it. So, he decided he would run the wiring himself through the attic and down the wall. I guess, when he was up there, he stepped where he shouldn't, or tripped, I don't know what, but he fell through the sheetrock and landed on his head on the garage floor. Broke his neck."

"Oh my god," Katie said. I could see her eyes wide in the low light. "That's...that's..."

I swallowed hard. "We—my mom and my brother and me—had left to go to the mall for back to school shopping or something. When we came home, my mom opened the garage door and we found him lying there. He was already blue. He was gone."

Thinking about it, remembering that scene, it was always hard. I had blocked it from my mind for the longest time. I could feel my chin trembling. Katie reached out and took my hand. It was warm, her touch soft.

"After that, there was this hole in the garage ceiling, right? For like a year. I would sometimes go out there and just stare at it. And my mom, she wouldn't even park her car in there. It stayed empty from then on. We eventually sold that house, moved into the one we live in now," I said.

"I had no idea," she said. "I am so sorry that happened to you." Her lip trembled now as she spoke.

"Hey," I said, trying to not only reassure her but to keep myself from breaking down, "like I said, it was a long time ago. I was just a kid. I don't even really remember much from that day, to be honest. Which, used to really bother me. I wanted to be able to remember the last thing he said to me, the last thing we had for breakfast together. But as I've gotten older, I've learned to let go of those things and remember the things he taught me. How the way he made me feel still shapes me today."

"Yeah, but being so young," she said.

"After he...after it happened, I didn't know what to do. None of us did, really. But then something happened one day. My mom, I guess she was having a bad day, so she pulled me out of school early while my brother was at football practice, and she took me to see the special edition of *Star Wars*. It was the most amazing thing I had ever seen in my life. After that, I poured myself into my art, into creating comics. I became obsessed with those movies. I mean, Luke Skywalker, his dad was dead too, right? I saw myself in this incredible hero character. So yeah, it sucks, but there's a part of me that wonders what my life would be like now. It was a way to cope, I know, but now, would this life even be what it is? Would it be better? I have no idea, but I do know it wouldn't be the same."

"Your mom never remarried?" she asked.

I laughed. "No way," I said. "No, she has spent all her time focused on me and my brother. I guess my dad's life insurance policy didn't really pay for much and she was suddenly a single mom with a single income."

"How old is he? Your brother?"

"He's two years older than me. He still lives at home, and I give him shit for it all the time, but honestly, I know it's because he doesn't want to leave mom. He knows I'm going off to art school, and he doesn't want to leave her by herself," I said.

My eyes fell to the space between my legs. I thought about all the times I'd chewed on the corner of my thumbnail, bit it until it would bleed. That anxious reaction to not being able to cope with the things around me. The nervousness of moving away from home for the exact reason that my brother couldn't make himself leave. "It makes me feel selfish."

"There's nothing selfish about pursuing what you want in life," Katie said. Then she nudged me again. "Hey, look at me."

I did, pulling me eyes to hers.

"You don't owe anyone your future, alright? When it comes to what you want to do and who you want to be, *you* only answer to *you*."

I nodded and she looked back to the ocean in front of us.

"Like I told you back in St. Louis, my parents divorced when I was really little," Katie said. "And I know that's not the same, and I'm not saying it because I want you to feel sorry for me or feel like I'm trying to say that I understand you because I grew up without both parents. Because that would be shitty. What I am trying to say, though, is that those things do create who we are. So I get that. Would I be sitting on a beach a thousand miles from home right now if I wasn't forced to spend a week every summer with my mom's sister? Probably not."

As she spoke, I watched her lips move, watched her eyes as they stared out at the darkness in front of us. "But I'm glad you are," I said.

She turned to me, sitting so close that I could see the reflection of myself in her dark irises. "Me too."

Then, she stood up, pulled off her shirt, tossed it a few

yards back onto the dry sand and turned back to me. "Want to go swim?"

Now, in that moment, what I *wanted* to say was, "Of course!" In my imagination, in that split-second, I would have stood up and tore my shirt off as well and ran into the soft surf, wade out into the cool water.

Instead, I said, the hesitancy in my voice thick, "In the dark?"

She rolled her eyes. "Yes, in the dark. Come on, it'll be fun. How many times will we get the chance to do this?"

I stood up and reluctantly removed my shirt and chinos, walking out in just my boxers, feeling overexposed. I tried not to stare at Katie, who had shed her jeans and was now walking into the water in just her underwear as well.

I expected the water to be much colder, but it was comfortable as we waded out further into the soft waves. I felt my footing in the sand, unsure at first, become more stable. At one point, Katie stumbled on something and started to fall over, but I caught her, my hands on her waist.

She turned to me, and I could have kissed her in that moment and it would have been perfect. And for a split-second, I thought she was leaning in, too. She tilted her head, almost like an invitation. Instead, she pulled back from me and said, "I'm sorry, Josh. I like you, I really do. And I know this sucks, but I can't get involved right now."

I hid my disappointment with a sly grin. "So you like me, huh?"

"More than I should admit," she said after a second's hesitation.

She started back for the shore, but I held onto those words.

That was, in my book, an absolute win.

CHAPTER 24

I WOKE UP WITH SAND IN MY HAIR AND MY FACE almost buried in the sleeping bag. My body felt stiff as I sat up to stretch, my hands sinking into the cool sand.

As I opened my eyes, I rolled to one side and saw Katie there, still wrapped in a sleeping bag borrowed from Hannah. She was close enough for me to wrap my arm around her and part of me wished that she had nuzzled up even closer during the night.

Joel and Hannah, on the other side of the pit we'd dug for the bonfire, were cuddled up together, his arm draped over her waist.

I remembered joining Katie in the water last night, my hands on her waist as she almost fell, pulling her close. In that split-second, I thought that she was going to kiss me and just the thought of it made me shiver with electricity.

After our swim, I had pulled off my saltwater-soaked boxer shorts and slept only in my chinos, and I could feel them chafing against my skin, bringing me back to the reality that we needed to get cleaned up before we piled into the Falcon and headed back into Agloe.

"Guys," I said. "We have to get up."

"What time is it?" Dustin asked groggily.

Though last night had been fun, it was apparent that none of us really got much sleep, and what we did get was restless anyway.

I found my Timex watch in the side pocket of my backpack. "It's just after seven," I said.

"Damn," Dustin said. "I wish we had another hour."

"I don't know about that," Katie said. "I don't think I can put up with this sand for another hour." She sat up in the sleeping bag, her hair wild and hanging around her face in sand-filled clumps.

"We've got to find somewhere to clean up," I said.

"Yeah," Dustin said, wiping sand from his arms and shaking it out of his hair. "Maybe sleeping on the beach wasn't the best idea we've ever had."

"No," I said. I glanced at Katie, who gave me the slightest of smiles. "It was a great idea." Her smile grew somewhat wider.

Joel and Hannah both woke up to the sound of us starting to stir.

"Good morning," Hannah said groggily. "Which one of you is the snorer?"

I gulped, but Katie shrugged. "I tried to warn you," she said.

We cleared up our little camping space, people starting to fill out on the beach, walking along the shoreline or jogging as the surf rolled in. Boats out on the water bobbed with the waves and an airplane flew overhead with a banner advertising a local restaurant floating behind it.

"I wish we could spend more time here," Hannah said as we packed the trunk of the car. She gestured to the rising sun. "This was almost worth the entire trip."

"Come on, guys," Dustin said. "We've only got a couple of hours before Mr. Reynolds lands. We need to go find this estate sale and get the action figure before that happens."

"Can we stop somewhere first?" Katie said. "I literally have beach in my teeth."

I decided that our best option would be one of the large travel stations that hugged the highway close by. They generally had large bathrooms with sinks where we could quickly scrub off any sand and wash our hair and brush our teeth.

Just a few miles away from the beach, I pulled into the parking lot of TravelCenter.

"Okay, let's make it quick," Dustin said. "We have almost an hour's drive back to Agloe."

Inside the travel center's bathroom, Joel, Dustin and I all huddled around the basin sinks, cleaning up from the night before. I smelled the worst, the seawater still on my skin. After about twenty minutes though, and with a fresh application of deodorant, I felt semi-decent and presentable.

We bought some donuts and coffee and were back on the highway, driving toward our destination.

"You said the estate sale was advertised in a newspaper, right?" I asked Dustin, who sat in the passenger seat next to me as I drove.

"Yeah," he said with a mouthful of powered donut. He washed it down with a plastic bottle of chocolate milk.

"Do you remember which date?"

"No," he said. "At least within the last week or so I would think."

"So we need to find a newspaper somewhere then."

He nodded. "I should have grabbed the copy that I made from Mr. Reynolds's printout."

"It's all good," I said. "If the estate sale is today, it'll be in the most recent edition." I had some experience with a sale like this. Before we moved from the old house, the one that my dad lived in, my mom held an estate sale, choosing to sell almost everything we owned and start over. At the time, I was angry that she would do that. But as I got older, I understood why she had to do it.

"Okay. Where would we find a newspaper?"

I gave him a wink. "I know just the place."

We arrived in the Agloe city limits, an hour from the beach and I pulled the Falcon into the parking lot of the one place I knew that would have all the most recent copies of the local newspaper: The Agloe City Library.

The library was in a building opposite of a strip center. Its yellow brick looked older than everything around it, as if it refused to be taken down in order to have some new shop built in its place.

"How did you know where the library was?" Joel asked from the backseat.

"I just had a hunch," I said. "Most small town libraries are in or near the downtown district."

"Well you're a genius," he said.

Dustin peered out the windshield. "Are they even open?"

"Sign says they open at eight," I said, pointing to the front doors. The hours of operation were there in white vinyl letters.

"Well, what are we waiting for?" Dustin said, popping open the door. "Let's go find some newspapers."

The five of us walked in the front doors and into the open building of bookshelves. Hints of wood and leather filled my nostrils. It reminded me of the library I'd grown up in, a few blocks from our old house in Greenwood. After my dad died, I spent almost every afternoon there, finding solace in books and comics, finding anything I could that had the Star Wars logo on it.

Inside the entrance was a rack of newspapers. We attacked it, all five of us, trying to find the most recent ones and flipping through the pages.

"It wouldn't be in the obits, right?" Dustin said, though I got the feeling he was talking to himself more than to the rest of us.

"Garage sales," Hannah said. "Find the garage sales section."

"I don't have a garage sales section," Joel said, tossing his newspaper down and grabbing another.

I flipped through the pages of the newspaper I had grabbed, looking past the sports section and scanning the headings for local events.

"Good morning," a woman said from the checkout desk. She was older, Hispanic, with jet black hair tied back in a ponytail. She had a magazine splayed open on the counter and a pair of wayfarers rimmed her eyes. "Is there something I can help you find?"

"Hi. We need the newspapers that show recent estate sales," I said as we approached the counter. It was U-shaped, jutting out into the relatively small common area of the library. I was already comfortable here though.

"Specifically estate sales that are happening today," Dustin quipped.

"Right," I said.

"All of the newspapers and other circulars that we have should be at that rack," the woman said. "Do you happen to know which estate sale in particular you're looking for? I can help you narrow it down a little bit."

"We don't know the address," Dustin said, "but I'm pretty sure it was in last Sunday's paper."

"And we know they have a lot of Star Wars stuff that we are interested in buying," Joel said.

"Ah," the woman said, taking off her glasses. "That's Bill Surber's widow, Jan. I can tell you exactly where that is."

CHAPTER 25

We all huddled around the desk that the librarian stood behind.

"You know what we're talking about?" Dustin asked.

"Of course I do," the librarian said. "Bill was not only a huge *Star Wars* fan, but he owned The Table's Edge."

"What's that?" I asked.

"It's the comic book shop over on the far end of Main Street. He always had the coolest stuff in there. I know a lot of the kids here, if the library didn't have a specific graphic novel, Bill would order it just for them to keep on his shelves. The kids loved him. His store was always a safe place for them to go."

We all nodded, knowing exactly what she meant. It sounded like The Table's Edge was the same sort of idea Dustin and Joel had for their store—a refuge more than a shop. A place that everyone would feel at home.

"When Bill died, Jan tried to keep the shop going as long as she could, but it just wasn't her strong suit. Plus I think it pained her to see it without him. That store, their customers, they were like his family, their family. She sold the shop to some national chain, and it's just not the same," she said. "And I think she's ready to move on."

Then she looked at us as if we finally came into focus. "Where are you all from?" The words came out slowly, like we were from some foreign place.

"Indiana," Joel said. "We drove here from Indiana."

"Goodness," she said. "How far was that?"

"About a thousand miles. Two days," I said.

"You're far from home then. Did you kids drive all this way just for Jan's estate sale?"

"Yes," Dustin said.

"And we're on a bit of a time crunch," I said. "There'a particular bunch of action figures that we want to buy."

"I can call Jan and see if she still has them," the librarian said with a shrug, and my heart leapt in my chest.

I could tell all of us were trying to remain calm, to not give off the fact that the action figure we were looking for was the difference in all of us being able to make our dreams come true or not.

"That," I said, "would be great. If you have time. You wouldn't mind?"

"Not at all." The woman brought a phone to her ear and dialed a number even as we spoke.

The five of us waited for a few moments that seemed to stretch on for eternity. Sweat collected under my armpits and I felt the nervousness ripple through my arms and down my spine. I glanced over at Katie, who was bouncing her foot nervously. Hannah had her bottom lip between her teeth. All of us, waiting on this phone call that had the potential of informing us that we'd driven all this way for nothing.

"Hey Jan," the woman said. She gave us a look that indicated that the person on the other end—this Jan—had picked up. "It's Stella over at the library. Listen, I have some kids here that drove all the way from Indiana looking for your estate sale." She then took the receiver away from her ear. "What exactly was it you all were wanting?"

"The action figures," Dustin said. "The *Star Wars* action figures. The lot was listed for two hundred and fifty dollars."

The librarian—Stella, we just learned—repeated this information.

"Okay, thank you so much. I'll send them your way." She hung up the phone.

"Okay, Jan said she still has them, but if you want them, you should get over there as soon as possible. She said she's had a few calls about them already," she said.

I could have hugged that woman right then and there. My heart was beating faster than it ever had before, and I tried to keep my composure. I could tell my friends were all having a similar reaction.

"Do you happen to know the address?" Dustin asked.

"Yes I do." Stella pulled a notepad with the City of Agloe letterhead on it and wrote it down.

"It's really only just a few blocks from here," she said. With the pencil, she drew a rudimentary map. "Just go to the stoplight at Pollard Street and make a left. It'll be at the corner of Pollard and 18th. If you get to the playground, you've gone too far."

"Thank you," we all said, almost in unison.

"You're welcome. Hope you find what you're looking for."

So did I.

So did all of us.

We couldn't leave the library fast enough, the five of us trying to get out the door at the same time. Once in the parking lot, Dustin jumped in the air and gave out a whoop of excitement, pumping his fist in the air.

"Did you hear that? She has them, *she has them*!" He bounced on his feet, giddy, like a child on Christmas morning.

Joel grabbed Dustin around the waist and picked him up off the ground, jumping around as well.

"Let's go! We have to hurry!" Joel exclaimed, finally letting Dustin down.

We piled back in the car. Katie took the passenger seat and she was smiling. We had done it. We made it, and now we were just a few blocks away from the estate sale, where our treasure was waiting for us.

Once we were all in the car, I shoved the key in the ignition and turned.

The engine whirred, puttered and shut off.

"No," I said. "No, no, no." I turned the key again and the Falcon still refused to start.

"What the hell is going on?" Dustin asked, his head poking through the space between the two front seats.

"I don't know! It won't start." I turned to Katie for any advice, hoping she had some insight as she had with the failed alternator on my Jeep.

"Pop the hood," she said.

Fumbling for the latch, I finally found it and pulled. The hood made a loud pop as it released. Katie jumped out and opened it up. After a few moments, she shut it again.

"Okay, try it now."

I turned the key and the car whined in protest once again. Then, just as I was about to give up, Joel reached up and punched the dash with his fist.

The Falcon roared to life.

"Ha!" he shouted. "I can't believe that worked! That actually worked!"

"Get in," I said to Katie, who jumped back in and shut her door.

"The negative battery terminal feels a little loose. We can tighten it up later," she said. "After we get what we came for."

"If it works, then it works," Hannah said from the center seat in the back.

Then I looked into the rearview mirror at the elation in my friend's faces. I pulled the stalk, putting the car in drive and accelerated into the street.

"Alright, guys," I said, "Let's go get rich."

CHAPTER 26

I DIDN'T NEED TO KNOW WHICH HOUSE THE ESTATE sale was at because when we pulled up, there were cars lining the street. I saw people walking up the sidewalk and toward a red brick house with wooden shutters around the windows. Though the garage doors were closed, there were several tables lining the driveway and in the lawn. There was a front porch, with two wooden rocking chairs facing the street. They had *for sale* signs on them.

I found an empty spot on the curb a few houses down and parked the Falcon. We got out of the car, and my nervousness was firing in overdrive. There were a lot of things in life that felt like miracles, but the fact that we made it here, that we'd not only survived, but arrived relatively unscathed, made this feel like something more than a teenage roadtrip. It felt like destiny, a true quest.

Dustin led us to the front door, Joel and Hannah behind him and Katie and I holding back a few steps.

"You alright?" I asked her, sensing some hesitation in her.

"Yeah," she said, but I could tell there was something off. She had been strangely quiet since the library. After fiddling with the battery cable or whatever she'd done under the hood of the Falcon, she had not said much.

"You can be honest with me, you know. What's going on?"

"We go in there and buy this action figure, and that's it. That's the end. I don't know, I'm sure it sounds stupid, but part of me was hoping that this trip would somehow go for eternity, that we would never have to return to our normal, boring, terrible lives," she said. "We do this, we go back and then what? I have this feeling that nothing will ever top sleeping on a beach under the stars. Nothing will be like seeing the Falcon for the first time. I don't know, I feel like I'm being nostalgic for something that hasn't even passed."

"Hey," Dustin poked his head out the door. "You guys coming or what?"

"Yeah," I said. Then I turned back to Katie. There were a thousand things I wanted to say in that moment. I wanted to tell her how I couldn't stop thinking about last night, swimming in the ocean. That this roadtrip didn't have to be the last that we spent time together.

She stared at me with those caramel-colored, almond-shaped eyes that I'd lost myself in several times over the last two days, as if she could read my mind.

"What?" she asked.

Dustin whistled at us and I nodded to Katie as we walked in, holding the door behind her.

"Ask me again sometime," I said.

I understood exactly what she meant, how these last two days somehow felt like another life entirely. Once we got back to Greenwood, we would have to face the reality of our regular lives. She would go back home to Chicago. There was a part of me that still couldn't grasp with the idea that we finally reached our destination.

Inside, there were people, mostly older people, scanning items for sale, checking price tags. There were tables set up with clothes and personal items that looked like they belonged to an older gentleman.

A wave of sadness came over me, knowing that what we were seeing was something I'd witnessed before—this was a widow who was trying to move on with life after the passing of her spouse.

"Are you okay?" Katie asked.

"Yeah," I lied. There was a lump in my throat.

We followed Dustin into another room, and I gasped. This room was a Star Wars shrine, the biggest collection of memorabilia I had ever seen. My jaw dropped. There were posters on the walls from the original movies. There were tables lining one of those walls with books, toys and other novelties.

"Oh my god," I said. "This is all incredible."

Dustin went to one of the shelves and held up a khaki-colored baseball cap with a blocked off logo patch on the front. I recognized the logo from Star Wars lore.

"He's got *Blue Harvest* stuff," he said, almost reverently.

"What's Blue Harvest?" Katie asked.

"It was the fake filming title of *Return of the Jedi*," Dustin said. "And look at this." He pointed to a movie poster with the title *Revenge of the Jedi*. That had been the original title of *Return of the Jedi* before it was changed at the last minute.

"I am just in awe," Joel said. He held up a lightsaber hilt. He read off the tag and put it back down on the table. "That's an actual prop from *Empire*, man," he said. "Luke Skywalker himself held that saber. This is like a religious experience."

I felt the same way. There was no way to see all this stuff and not feel like we'd walked into some holy place.

Against the far wall, there was a pinball machine twinkling with lights. I wanted to play it. I wanted to take it home. I wanted all of it. This room was my childhood dreams all realized.

"Yeah, but—where are the figures?" Hannah asked as she scanned the items in on the tables.

She was right. They weren't in here. Had we missed them? Or had someone swooped in right before we arrived and taken off with them? I could feel anxiety creeping up in my spine.

"Can I help you all find something?" a woman's voice asked from the doorway.

We turned to see a woman with a bob of greying blonde hair walk into this room, standing in the doorway.

She watched us with intrigue and curiosity. Her eyes were light blue and lightly lined, though kind. Kind, but sad.

"Hi," Dustin said. "We actually came from the library. Stella, I think was her name," he started, but the woman cut him off.

"Oh yes. You all are here for the action figures, is that correct?" she said.

"Yeah," Dustin said. "Uh, yes ma'am."

"You guys must be really big Star Wars fans," she said. "Stella said you drove all the way from Illinois?"

"Indiana," I said. "But, yes ma'am."

"I'm not even going to begin to ask how you found out about Bill's collection."

"The internet," Dustin said. "We, uh, check the internet a lot for collectibles for sale."

"That's so incredible," she said. "Someday there won't even be physical newspapers, everything will be published directly on the internet." She said this mostly to herself than to us. Then she turned her attention back to Dustin. "Follow me, I pulled them out of here, since Stella told me you were on your way."

I exhaled, not realizing that I had been holding my breath.

We followed the woman out of the Star Wars room and back into what I thought was the home's living room. Most of the furniture in here had either been packed away, though there was still a couch and a chair—both with handwritten *sold* signs on them.

"Are you Jan?" Hannah asked.

"Yes I am," the woman said.

"I'm so sorry for your loss. All of us are."

Jan turned and gave us a warm smile. "That's very sweet. Thank you."

"Your husband must have been a huge Star Wars fan," Hannah said.

"Oh goodness," Jan said. "Those movies were his entire life. He loved them and all the stuff that came with it. I'm pretty certain he opened the comic shop just to have the excuse to buy more."

"Well," Dustin said, "he had great taste."

"He would have taken that as a nice compliment."

Then, from behind a folding table that was adorned with a black tablecloth and a bank bag with her sale cash, she heaved a cardboard box.

"Here it is," Jan said. "The box of action figures. I guess Bill never got around to stocking these at the store, and since I already sold that place I didn't want to take them over there."

We gathered around the box. There were Luke Skywalkers and Darth Vaders and Obi-Wan Kenobis, all in retail packaging from the original run that Kenner toys made back in the late-70's.

And there, packed in with them, was the one we'd come for.

I could barely contain myself, and I felt my fingers go numb. My friends, I could tell, were all having a similar reaction.

"May I?" Dustin asked, gesturing to the box. "I'd like to check this one out."

"Yes, of course," the woman said nonchalantly. Then, across the room, someone else asked a question and Jan, turning back to us, said, "I'll be right back. Take your time with them."

Dustin reached in, his hand visibly shaking and pulled the Boba Fett from the rest of the figures. In person, the packaging was even more surreal. The card backing was adorned with the Star Wars logo in silver. To the right of it, an animated Luke Skywalker held a lightsaber high above his head. And there, in the plastic bubble glued to the cardboard, was the Boba Fett figure itself. Standard action figure size, three-and-three-quarter-inches, it was in perfect condition. The rocket on its back was intact.

We huddled around Dustin, almost too close, as he held it. My breathing was labored and uneven. My heart pulsed heavily in my chest.

"This is it," Dustin said. Tears streaked down his cheeks. "This is really it."

"Can I hold it?" Joel asked.

Dustin gingerly handed it over and Joel cradled the retail box in his hands like it was a delicate creature and not a toy.

"I can't believe it," he said. "I just..."

"Yeah," Hannah said, resting her head on his shoulder.

"We drove all this way," I finally said. "And part of me still had this thought in the back of my mind that it wasn't the real thing, that we'd been duped or we'd been mistaken."

"This is the real deal." Joel could barely get the words out, his voice shaking. "This is really it. Oh my god."

"Plus," Dustin said in a half-whisper, "look at the rest of this stuff. This isn't just regular action figures. There's some other rare stuff in here. Guys, this is a goldmine. Whoever this lady's husband was, he knew what he was holding onto."

Hannah had tears streaming down her face now too, and she held onto Joel, wrapping her hands around his arm and leaning against him. "This is our ticket to our own place," she whispered. "I just can't believe it."

"It's sad that she doesn't know what she has," Katie sort of whispered. "I mean, to her, these are just toys."

Jan returned to the table and we all tried to collect ourselves. "Sorry about that. One of the tables over there didn't have a price marker. Anyway, everything look alright?"

"Yes," Dustin choked out. "And the newspaper said the lot of figures was two-fifty?"

"Yes, I think so," she said. On the table, she flipped through a notebook. "Yes, there it is. Box of action figures. Retail price individually is about seven dollars per figure at our store, so I rounded down a little."

"That seems fair," Dustin said.

"I've had a few people call about some of this stuff, but I'm glad you all are taking them to be honest. I know Bill would love to see this all go to real fans like yourselves and not just some other comic shop owner or someone trying to make a quick buck."

"We are," Joel said. "Real fans, I mean."

"Big fans," Dustin said.

"Well, I just need payment and then you can take them," Jan said.

Dustin nodded to me, and I reached in my back pocket to grab my wallet, to hand over the cash, to make the transaction. My hands shook as I produced the bills and handed them over.

Then, just as she reached out to take the money from my hand, the front door opened. Light spilled in, and a figure cut a dark hole in the pillar of brightness.

"Dustin?" a man's voice said. Then, more angrily, "No!"

We all turned. Mr. Reynolds stood in the doorway, his eyes on the box of action figures and the cash in my hand. And in that moment, with my heart in my throat, with my hands slick with sweat, we knew that *he* knew that he'd been double-crossed.

CHAPTER 27

"What is going on here?" Mr. Reynolds asked. "Why are you..." he trailed off, the confusion on his face slowly transforming into anger.

"I'm sorry," Jan said. "Who are you, sir?"

Mr. Reynolds collected himself and flashed a smile, his false teeth bright and sparkling. He dressed up for the occasion, too, wearing a black button up, untucked, and a blazer that hung from his skinny frame like it was still on a hanger and not on a body. "Hi," he said. "My name is Jeff Reynolds. And you must be Jen, correct? We spoke on the phone a few days ago."

The five of us stood between them. I held my head low, knowing that we were most certainly in trouble. Dustin was surely fired now.

"It's Jan," she said. "Jan Surber. And yes, you're from the comic book store in..." she trailed off.

"Greenwood, Indiana," he said.

Jan looked at us, and I saw the realization strike her that we were from the same place.

"Do you kids know this man?" she asked us.

We nodded sheepishly.

"Yes ma'am," Dustin said.

"Mrs. Surber. *Jan*. I think I can explain what is going on here," Mr. Reynolds said. "You see, this young man works for me." He gave Dustin a quick glance, his eyes narrow. Dustin looked away in shame, his cheeks flush. "He must have seen the information for your estate sale—which, I am so sorry for your loss." The way he said this sounded as sincere as a kick to the shin. He continued, "And I am assuming he and his...*friends* took it upon themselves to come down here and swindle you out of them."

"Swindle?" Jan said, almost incredulous. "I guess I am not following you. These kids came here and gave me exactly what I was asking for these figures. They didn't even haggle on the price. There's no swindling here."

"Oh, but I'm afraid there is," Mr. Reynolds said. "You see, I am a collector, much like your late husband. I know what I am looking for and I search the internet every week for estate sales just like this one, in hopes that I can rescue under-appreciated items from falling into unscrupulous hands. I travel all across the country searching for rare and collectible items."

Jan looked to us. "Is this true?"

"Yes," Dustin said.

"But these are just toys," Mrs. Surber said. "My husband stocked this stuff in our shop all the time. There's nothing special about them. And I'm not sure I am comfortable selling them to someone who obviously makes a living by purchasing items at estate sales and reselling them for profit."

"You don't understand, Mrs. Surber. I am willing to offer a substantial sum for the entire lot." Mr. Reynolds reached into the breast pocket of his jacket and produced a checkbook. "I am prepared to write a check for five thousand dollars for the action figures."

My stomach dropped. Dustin gasped and took a step toward Mr. Reynolds, coming between the man and Jan.

"No!" Dustin said. "You can't do that! We got here first."

"It doesn't matter who got here first, it's who offers the most money. And knowing your weekly wages, I am confident that this won't be a problem for me," Mr. Reynolds said. He then returned his attention to Jan. "Now, do we have a deal?"

Jan paused for a moment, seeming to measure his words. She looked from him to the box of figures and back up.

"How about ten thousand? I can write you a check for ten thousand dollars right now," Mr. Reynolds pressed.

Dustin seethed. Joel and Hannah were both stunned. And Katie, next to me, glared at the comic shop owner. I gulped, because I could see what she was thinking in her eyes. We couldn't let him outspend us, but we had no choice.

Actually, I had *one* choice.

I turned and went to Mrs. Surber, coming between her and Mr. Reynolds. Her eyes were still sad. I could see tears starting to form in the corners.

"You can't sell these to him," I said. I pushed the box of action figures toward her, sliding them on the surface of the table. "In fact, you can't sell them to us either."

"Dude," Dustin whispered. "What are you doing?"

I ignored him, reached in the box and pulled out the Boba Fett. "This isn't just an action figure, ma'am. This is a one of a kind collectible."

I then turned to Mr. Reynolds, whose eyes had gone wide with the certainty that he'd lost out here. I held the figure up at eye level. "This action figure alone is worth well over a hundred thousand dollars, and he knows that, too. That's why he's offering you so much. But more than that, you simply can't sell it." I leaned closer to Jan and placed the Boba Fett in her hands. "Because this stuff is more valuable than just money, and I think you know that."

The widow looked down at the box and back up at me. Her lip trembled, a single tear dripped down her cheek. Then, as that tear fell from her cheek and dampened the carpet between her feet, she looked up at Mr. Reynolds. "I need you to leave, sir."

"Ma'am, that figure is highly inflated," he said, his words quick, almost stumbling out of his mouth, "but nonetheless, I am willing to offer—"

She cut him off, "I said *leave*. These aren't for sale. Nothing is." Then, she turned. "Karen," she said. A woman, working another table, another cash drawer, turned to Mrs. Surber. "Will you escort this man out? In fact, the whole sale is closed for the day."

The woman, Karen, came over to the table. She glanced at us, at Mr. Reynolds and at the box of action figures. "Is everything alright?" she asked quietly. "Do I need to call the authorities?"

Mrs. Surber turned toward us, almost as if she were giving us a once-over. "I don't believe so. But please escort this man," she nodded to Mr. Reynolds, "and everyone else out. These five, though, they can stay."

Mr. Reynolds took a step toward us, and we instinctively moved back. He glared down at Dustin. "You," he said, "are obviously fired."

"I'm pretty sure that was a given," Dustin said.

"Don't be sarcastic," he spat. "You have ruined everything. Do you know how much I have invested in searching for this figure? Do you know how much I had on the line here?"

"Sir, I think it's time to leave," Karen said, coming in between Mr. Reynolds and us.

"This is...this is outrageous! I will have my attorney get in contact," he said, turning to the front door. Mr. Reynolds walked out, huffing, allowing the door to slam shut behind him. Others left as well, confusion in the air as they murmured about the estate sale as they walked out.

And I couldn't help but feel like I had ruined more than just Mr. Reynolds' purchase. My friends and I had so much riding on this sale, and now we stood in this woman's living room, empty handed and—for Dustin and myself—jobless.

Jan and Karen went to the front door and escorted the last of the stragglers out, a confused murmur rippling through the dozen or so people as they left.

"Dude," Dustin said as we all huddled together. The word was stretched out and I could hear the disappointment in his voice. "What do we do now? We lost."

"I'm sorry." I took in all of my friends, the despair on their faces. "I just couldn't do it," I said. "I couldn't allow Mr. Reynolds to take off with that figure, to flash his cash and outbid us. We all know what he was going to do with it. He would sell it immediately just to make himself richer."

"Don't pretend to be the moral compass here," Dustin said. He was clearly angry. "What did you think we were going to do? Hold onto it? Play with it? No. We were going to sell it too!"

"Josh is right, though," Katie said. "We were going to use it to change our lives. Mr. Reynolds was trying to take advantage of that lady just to put more money in his pocket. You guys were going to start your business. Josh was going to pay for his tuition."

"I agree with Josh," Joel said. "I would rather no one buy it than see Mr. Reynolds strong-arm his way into getting it."

Dustin relented. "I know," he finally said, sighing. He leaned against a wall. "I just...don't know what to do now."

"None of us do. But," I said, "we did the right thing."

He nodded slowly. "Yeah. You're right, Josh. We did."

Jan returned to the living room after all the people had been escorted out. "Okay," she said. "Why don't you all have a seat?" She gestured to the living room furniture. "I'm going to pour some lemonade and then I need someone to explain to me exactly why this toy is worth so much money."

It was weird, sitting on furniture with for sale signs on them, price tags on bright, neon-colored stickers on the cushions. Still, we sat together, huddled on the couch, the five of us crunched together on the three cushions. Jan had offered us all lemonade and we drank out of glass tumblers.

"First," she said, "how exactly did you find out about this estate sale? You said the internet?"

"Well, from a certain point of view. Mr. Reynolds was telling the truth," Dustin said. "I work—well, worked, I guess—for him. He owns a comic book shop in Greenwood, Indiana, where we're from. I saw a print-out of the estate sale on his desk after the weekend and saw the picture of the action figures. I knew what I was looking at almost immediately. That Boba Fett is the most famous action figure of all time."

"You act like it's the only one or something," Jan said, her eyes narrowed.

"It is," Joel said. "It's what we call the king of action

figures. There was only one ever made with retail packaging, and your husband had it. Now you have it."

She looked away for a moment, out the window, the mini blinds open, and then she laughed. Low at first and then a hearty, full-on belly laugh. We all looked at each other, not knowing what was going on.

Finally after a few moments, the widow collected herself. "I'm sorry," she said, wiping tears from her eyes with the back of her hand. "But I just know that my Bill is cursing at me from heaven knowing that I was about to sell all this stuff for the price that he told me he paid for it."

CHAPTER 28

After thirty minutes or so, we had become comfortable talking with Jan, and told her about all our plans and how we schemed to get to Agloe before Mr. Reynolds did, to beat him to the purchase. She listened to our story intently, finding it humorous at points.

"We made a plan that we would drive down here and buy it before Mr. Reynolds could. Originally, we were hoping to be here yesterday, to buy it and be back on the road before he even flew in. But that didn't work out," I said.

"We took a wrong turn," Dustin said. "We ended up in St. Louis, even though we meant to go to Memphis. This crazy guy at a comic book shop there—"

Jan cut him off. "Ah. You met Yoda."

"You know Yoda?!" we all exclaimed, almost in unison.

"We used to see him at conventions. A..." she raised her eyes to the ceiling for a moment, as if looking for the right words, "strange character."

"Well, he tried to take our car, but Josh won a card tournament. But then our car broke down," Dustin continued.

"Then, this mechanic in Little Rock let us take his Falcon," Hannah said.

"You kids have had quite an adventure," she said.

"I guess you could say that," I said.

"I mean, I get that this figure, you say it's worth all this money. What were you all going to do with it? You must have had some kind of plan if it was worth coming all the way."

"We were going to sell it at a comic convention or an auction," Dustin said.

"Get our own place," Hannah said.

"Start our own comic book shop," Joel said.

"I was going to pay my tuition," I said.

There was a long moment of silence. "Huh," the widow said. "Sounds like you all were banking a lot of your future on this."

"Yeah," I said, almost guiltily. But the truth was, that was exactly what we had done. The entire plan, not just for me, but for all of us, hinged on the action figure, of being able to buy it and flip it.

"My husband would have loved that. He loved a good adventure," she said.

She looked up at the wall, and I could see the dust outline of a picture frame. I imagined that's where their wedding photo hung, the way she stared at the empty space.

"And he would have loved your story. He had such a soft spot for our customers, who were mostly kids like yourselves. Driving across the country, sleeping on the beach? He would have eaten it up." Her eyes welled with tears again and she dabbed at them with a tissue, balling it up in her hand.

"I guess we owe you an apology," Hannah said.

"Nonsense," Jan said. "If anything, you kept me from making a terrible mistake. Not just selling the figure, but all of this. This was, for better or worse, my Bill's love. He genuinely loved Star Wars and we wouldn't have even had the comic book store if not for those movies. After he died, I guess I just wanted a fresh start. It was painful to look at all of this. So I asked my sister Karen to help me put together the estate sale. I would sell it all, sell the house and find something else."

"I know what you mean," I said sheepishly. "My dad died almost ten years ago. I watched my mom do the exact same thing. She sold everything we had and sold our house and we started all over."

She gave me an empathetic look. "Oh goodness. I'm so sorry."

"I say all the time that it was *a long time ago*, but there hasn't been a day go by that I haven't thought about him. And sometimes, I wish we still lived in that house, even if it was where he died. I wish we still had the chair he sat in," I said. "So I think you're doing the right thing by holding onto your husband's things."

"Thank you," Jan said. "So heartbreaking, but maybe the answer is in the holding on, not in the letting go."

Katie put her arm around me and let me lean against her shoulder.

"I do think I have an idea, though," Jan said slowly. "Would you all follow me to the garage?"

She stood up from the chair and led us through the house to the garage, which was just off the kitchen. She flipped on a light and hit a button that operated the overhead door. As light filled the space, what we saw was a well-known sight.

Rows and stacks of longboxes, the narrow storage boxes for comic books.

"This was his personal collection," Jan said. "All these boxes, stuff that he never took to the shop."

"Wow," Dustin said.

We echoed his sentiment. There had to be a hundred boxes in here, all of them stuffed full of comics.

"You kids want to open your own shop, right?" Jan said.

Dustin and Joel nodded to her.

"Well, you're going to need inventory." Jan cracked a wide smile.

"Are you saying..." Joel trailed off.

"Have at it," she said. "It's yours."

CHAPTER 29

Jan left us out there and we sat in the floor of the garage for what felt like hours, gawking over every single box and its contents. Just as soon as we thought we'd found something that floored us, in another box there was even more.

They were all labelled, too. On the lower corner of each box, a sticker had been applied with information on its contents. Publisher, dates, issues, everything, already cataloged.

"This is incredible," Dustin said, pulling open a box of Marvel's *Star Wars* run from the late-70s. "I have never seen these in person."

"Is that a giant green rabbit?" Katie asked, holding up one of the issues. On the cover was Han Solo, his blaster aimed straight at the reader. Behind him, Chewbacca and, to his right, a green rabbit in a red spacesuit. In hindsight, it was a ridiculous visual.

Dustin, Joel and I all giggled. "The early days of the

franchise were pretty wild," Joel said. "They were still trying to figure out exactly what *Star Wars* was."

I spent some time going through some old *Batman* comics while Katie had another box in front of her, going through *Spawn* issues. "This reminds me of my childhood," she said. "My mom would say I was too young to read this stuff, but my uncle would always bring me new issues anyway. I would read them at night, under the blankets. It was so stereotypical, reading after bedtime with a flashlight."

"I was the same way," I said. "Except it was *Star Wars* books and *Batman* comics."

"We would have gotten along great," she said, "if we had grown up together."

"We do now," I said.

Her eyes lit up. "Yeah. We do."

"How are we going to get all this back to Greenwood?" Hannah asked, a pile of longboxes stacked next to her. "There's not much room in the Falcon."

"I have no idea," Dustin said. "We might be able to get four boxes though."

"We're definitely going to have to come back," Joel said. "With a truck or something."

"Another trip?" I suggested.

"Why not? Look at all this. It's well worth it," Dustin said. "Then we're going to have to find a place to sell it all."

"Do we need a physical store?" Joel asked.

"What do you mean?" Dustin asked. "If we don't have

a store, how do we sell comics?"

"I was just thinking about all this, about how Mr. Reynolds finds estate sales online. What if instead of a physical shop, we have a website?" Joel said.

"We take pictures of the comics and load them on a website and take sales on the internet," Hannah said, thinking out loud. "That might actually work."

"There's no overhead that way," I said. "You can literally run it out of your apartment."

"We'd have to buy envelopes for shipping, but then our customer base just isn't limited to Greenwood," Joel said. "We can sell to anyone, anywhere."

"If people search for comic books online," Hannah said, "we would be their store."

"I like this," Dustin said. "And since we wouldn't have to rent a retail shop, we could charge less."

"We could literally sell what Mr. Reynolds sells for almost half the price," Joel said. Then he turned to me. "What do you think?"

"If I can get my weekly books for half the price, I'm your customer from day one!" I said.

"So it's settled," Joel said. "We're opening a comic book store—on the internet!"

After spending the rest of the morning and well into the afternoon in Jan's garage, we had packed five boxes—all that would fit in the Falcon—with the books we wanted the most and the things we thought would sell on the website. Even as we packed, Joel and Dustin talked nonstop about their idea and what the site would look like, brainstorming the entire operation together.

Katie sidled up next to me as I was putting some of the boxes back in their place. "You haven't said much. You alright?"

"Yeah," I said. I sat on the ground and looked through a few more comic books as I replaced them in their cataloged boxes.

"Hey," she said, kneeling next to me. "You did the right thing."

A raised eyebrow belied my ability to believe the statement.

Had I?

I mean, sure, we kept Mr. Reynolds from getting the action figures, kept him from taking advantage of Jan. But at the same time—we weren't leaving with what we thought we would either.

My friends hadn't said much to me in the last couple of hours. They animatedly discussed their plans for their online comic shop, but I knew just as much as they did—whether they'd admit it or not—that it was a contingency plan.

"Don't look at me like that," she said. "I can't speak for everyone but I know that I feel better leaving today like this than buying that action figure from her."

"We just had so much riding it," I said. "Now we're going home empty-handed."

"No we're not," she said. "We're leaving with full hearts."

"I can't pay my tuition with a full heart," I said. "I was really depending on this to work out." I finished packing the box and put the cardboard lid back on. "I have no idea what I'm going to do now."

"I believe good things come to people who do good things," Katie said.

I slid the last box back where I'd found it, next to a bunch of others, and stood up, dusting my hands off on my khakis. We were all dirty, covered in dust and even though we had a thousand miles to get home, I couldn't wait to get in the shower when we got there.

"You guys ready?" Dustin asked, coming up the driveway from the Falcon.

"Yeah," Katie said. "Just putting a few more back in storage."

"Joel and I have been talking. The comic con in Indy next month? We're going to rent a truck to come down to get the rest of this stuff before then and launch our store at the convention," he said. "Even if we opened a physical store like we originally thought, we would have never had this much inventory without coming here."

"I just feel like I ruined our plans," I said. "We came here for the Boba Fett, not all these comic books."

He took a few steps toward me and put his hands on my shoulders. "Dude, when I found that Boba Fett, you were the first person I told. Before I even told Joel, I ran to find you. Without you, we wouldn't even be here. It was your car that brought us, your smarts that rescued us in St. Louis. We owe the future of our comic shop wholly to you. And we'll make it up to you. I'm not sure how, but we will. I promise."

By this time, both Joel and Hannah, having packed the Falcon, had come up to the garage as well.

"He's right," Joel said. "This may not be what we planned, but I feel better about this than I did taking that Boba Fett."

"Seeing all that stuff, all those memories in that house," I said, trailing off. I couldn't finish the sentence. Tears streamed down my face and I buried my eyes in Katie's shoulder. She wrapped her arms around me, and my friends all hugged me as well.

I dried my eyes on the sleeve of my shirt. "I wish I still had some of my dad's stuff, you know? My mom, she was so quick to sell it all. And I get it. It was hard to look at. Hard to be in that house. But man, I miss seeing the things that he touched."

"And only you could have made that decision today," Joel said. "Dustin's right. This comic book store will be possible because you made the right call."

I smiled, though still heavy-hearted.

Once we put everything back in place, pulling the garage door shut, Jan met us at the car.

"You kids drive home safely, please," she said. "I would like a phone call when you get there."

"Thank you," Hannah said. "For all of this."

"Trust me," Jan said. "Bill would be ecstatic that all

this would be going to someone who appreciates it as much as he did. He would be over the moon to see you guys out here. I know that his legacy is in good hands."

She turned to me. "And thank you," she said. "For helping me see that I was making a huge mistake in selling or getting rid of all of his stuff. It has been too painful to see it all, but now I know differently—it's his lasting legacy that he left me with. That's worth more than I could ever sell this stuff for."

Jan then pulled me in for a hug, and for the second time, all my friends wrapped me in a group hug as well.

"You kids better get on the road," she said. "You've got a bit of a journey ahead of you."

After a few more goodbyes, we got in the Falcon and drove off, heading north, on our way to return the car to Lando before going home.

Katie only had to wiggle the battery terminal once.

CHAPTER 30

We took shifts driving back to Greenwood. Passing through Little Rock, we stopped by Lando's shop, where my Cherokee was sitting out front, waiting for us. He had even taken the time to wash it and vacuum it out.

When he asked about our trip and if we'd been successful in our journey, we told him the truth—that we'd willingly left the Boba Fett with its rightful owner. He seemed impressed with that and, as Chewbarka begged us for belly rubs, we transferred everything out of the Falcon, making sure it was clean and spotless before leaving Lando's shop. Since we didn't have to spend the last of our money on the action figures, we tried to give him the cash but he wouldn't take it.

We drove into Greenwood early the next morning, having driven through the night, taking four-hour shifts. The sun rose over the eastern skies, coming up in beautiful hues of pink and red. As I drove, I stole a glance or two at

Katie, who slept soundly in the passenger seat beside me, her head resting against the cool window. If I could, I would have continued driving, never wanting this trip to end. But it had to, and it did.

I dropped everyone off at Joel's apartment. Katie stopped me as I helped her with her bags.

"Hey," she said, holding my comic book in her hand. "Can I keep this?"

"Uh," I said. "Yeah, sure."

"Thank you. I know it's the original copy but I really like it."

"I might have some time over this next year to work on a new one," I said. "This trip has let me do a lot of thinking about the art institute and my future."

"Yeah?"

"I think it would be smart to just stay here for another year. I can work, save up some money and go next fall. Plus I'll be able to help Dustin and Joel with setting up their comic store. They'll need someone to catalogue all this stuff from Jan," I said.

"Well," Katie said, "don't sell yourself short. And when you get to Indy, look me up."

"I will."

We hugged and, after lingering for a second, she walked up the long driveway to the garage behind the house.

Then, I got back in my Jeep, put it in drive, and went home.

I SAT in Mr. Gilroy's tiny office, my hands clasped in my lap and trembling. I wore my nicest pair of chinos and a red polo shirt, hoping to look professional. I even combed my hair back, the locks falling behind my ears. I wanted nothing more than to tear at my thumbnail with my teeth, but I kept the urge at bay.

"I know I don't deserve it," I said. "And I know what I did was wrong, but this job is important to me. If you let me come back, I promise to not ever leave you stranded like that again."

He leaned back in the chair, listened to my story and my apology, then he leaned forward, his glasses sitting on the end of his nose.

"You left me without a shift manager," he said. As he spoke, he looked at me over the top of his glasses. His words weren't angry or annoyed, but they still stung. "I have to have employees that I can count on."

"I understand that," I said. "And if I had to be honest, being asked to be the store manager was not something I was anticipating, and I didn't know how to handle it. Because I'm not ready for that. I don't want that."

"Huh. I guess I was asking too much of you," he said. "I thought you had great potential. But I understand your apprehension. It's isn't for everyone."

"I plan on staying here for another year and then reapply to the Indianapolis Art Institute. But until then, if I could have my job back, it would help me out a lot."

He pushed the glasses up on his nose and, with his hands clasped on the desk in front of him, sighed.

“I’m,” he paused, thinking on his words. My stomach dropped. “I’m sorry, Josh. I’m going to have to stick with what I said here. I wish you luck for the future.”

I wanted to cry right there, but I steeled myself and stood up from the chair and shook his hand.

“Thank you for meeting with me today,” I said. “I appreciate your time.”

“And I appreciate you coming in to talk with me. That shows real maturity, but I think it’s clear that you don’t *belong* here.”

I gulped and cocked my head, not sure of what he meant.

“You’re meant for big things, Josh,” Mr. Gilroy said. “But those big things aren’t at Kaleidoscoops.”

“I understand.”

I left and, after my meeting with Mr. Gilroy, I went to see Dustin and Joel. I hadn’t seen them since we got back from Agloe, which was a week ago.

I walked up the steps to the apartment and knocked on the door.

“Come in!” I heard Joel call out.

When I opened the door, I was met with a pile of long-boxes stacked in the entryway. Both Joel and Dustin were sitting at a desktop computer, leaning over the desk. Joel had a stack of comic books in his lap and gave Dustin the details, who typed them into the system.

"Whoa," I said. "When did you guys get all these?"

"We made a deal with Jan," Joel said. "We had them shipped to us. In fact, we have something to show you." He nodded to Dustin. "Grab the papers."

Dustin got up from the desk and went over to our game table, which, usually covered with our Dungeons and Dragons books or other games, was littered with books like *Web Design for Dummies* and *The Idiot's Guide to Online Sales*. He grabbed a folder and brought it over to me.

"This is just a draft, but we think it's fair," he said.

"What is it?" I asked, taking the folder. Opening it up, I read the first few lines. It was their letters of incorporation.

"This is a real business," I said. "You guys are really doing this."

"Not just us," Dustin said. "Jan is going to be an investor. She thinks the future of collecting is on the internet. Guys like Mr. Reynolds have been keeping this a secret for so long, using the internet to find what they can and making a huge profit. We are going to bring that directly to the people."

As I continued reading, I stopped. "Wait," I said. "You're splitting the profits with me?"

"We are all in this together. The three of us from the very beginning and forever. But again, it's just a draft, and you don't have to sign it," Joel said. "We just want you to be involved."

"Especially when you become a big shot comic artist," Dustin said.

"Wow," I said.

"The three of us will be majority partners and Katie and Hannah each will have fifteen percent ownership," Joel said. "Jan will have ten percent."

I nodded, reading the papers.

"This is too much, guys. I don't deserve this," I said.

"No way," Dustin said. "We all deserve to be in charge of our own destiny."

"Where's Hannah?" I asked.

"She and her mother drove Katie back to Chicago. They're going through Indy and she's getting us a booth for the comic con while there," Joel said. "Jan pulled some strings for us. Since her husband's old store won't be there this year, there was an opening for a spot. We're trying to catalogue everything we got from her before then so we know what to price it all at. We're going to use the con to launch the store."

I looked over the papers once again, the name of the business catching my eye. "I like the name," I said.

"Good," Joel said. "We thought it was a fitting tribute."

The paper read *Chewie's Comics.*

"Well, I guess I should let you guys get back to work," I said.

Then, Dustin waved at me with one hand while putting the other to his temple. "You *will* help us catalogue these books."

I broke out into a wide grin. "I will help you catalogue these books."

"And you will get me a Mountain Dew."

"Hey now," I said, grabbing a box and carrying it to the desk. "Those tricks only work on the simple-minded."

CHAPTER 31

"What are you working on?"

My mom leaned over my desk, taking a look at the rough drafts of the drawings that I had scattered around. I had a lamp illuminated, the articulating arm bent and swiveled over my papers.

"That doesn't look like a comic book."

"It's not," I said. "It's a logo."

I had been drawing the new logo for our comic shop, working on different iterations for the last few weeks. I finally had a version I liked, settling on a cartoon-version of our favorite dog in Arkansas over a red ribbon that read *Chewie's Comics*.

"For your comic book shop?"

"Yeah," I said. I pulled my chair back and held the page up for her. "What do you think?"

"I like it."

"Thanks." I put the paper back down on the desk and

swiveled my chair around to face her. “Hey, can I ask you something?”

“Sure.”

“Do you ever wish you’d hung onto that house on Hughes Street? That we had stayed there, despite what happened to dad?”

She stepped away from the desk and sat on the edge of my bed. She looked out the window for a moment and sighed. “Sometimes,” she finally said, still staring out the window. Her hands clung to the edge of my mattress. I could see her grip loosen a bit after a moment. “Sometimes I think that I moved us out too fast, that I didn’t give myself time to grieve. That you boys had so much change over that year.”

“It’s weird because I have these false memories, you know?” I said. “And I know it doesn’t make sense, because he never lived here, right? But sometimes I walk in the kitchen and I swear that he used to sit in that breakfast nook.”

“I used to wake up every day, and would feel that he’s still right there. Or I would wash the sheets and swear I could smell his cologne on them before I placed them in the washer. Those memories are powerful,” she said.

“I used to be angry at you,” I said, my eyes going to my feet. “When I was little, when we moved into this house, I was so angry because we would never have memories of Dad here.”

She gulped.

I stood up and went across the room to sit next to her, taking her hand in mine. "But I understand now. How much those memories hurt for you, how much you wanted to leave them behind in that house. I get it."

"Thank you," she said as a single tear fell down her cheek, leaving a dark trail of mascara behind it. "All I wanted was to make sure you boys were alright."

I squeezed her hand. "We are," I said. "You did a great job."

From the hallway, the landline phone rang, and she stood up to go answer it. I went back to my drawing, but before I could continue to work, to put the finishing touches on it, she called my name.

"Yeah?" I said.

"There's some girl on the phone for you."

"Alright," I said.

I put down my pencil and walked into the hallway where we had a phone hanging on the wall. My mom gave me a look, her eyebrows dancing and, embarrassed, I turned away from her.

"Hello?" I said.

"Hey stranger." I recognized the voice immediately.

"Hey," I said. "How've you been? How did you get this number?"

"I have my sources," Katie said. "Which are really just Hannah and Joel. Anyway, what are you doing this weekend?"

"Actually," I said. "The comic con in Indy is this weekend. I'm going up there with Dustin, Joel and Hannah. We're launching the store at the con, using it as our grand opening."

"That's actually why I'm calling," she said. "I'm going to be there as well, hanging out with my uncle. I was hoping we could meet up."

"Yeah?" I asked, my heart giving a sudden flutter. I hadn't seen Katie since we got back from Agloe. I had looked her up on MySpace, but decided to keep things platonic between us. "I would like that. I would like to see you again."

"Perfect," she said. "I can't wait to see you either."

"Where should we meet up?"

"Are you guys staying at the convention center hotel?"

The con was held at a large convention center in downtown Indianapolis, with a hotel attached to it. Though we hadn't officially launched the store yet, we had received a few special orders of comic books from some local friends who were disenchanted with Mr. Reynolds and his prices. We had booked our rooms with the proceeds.

"Yes we are," I said.

"Also perfect. Okay, I'll see you there. Meet me at the hotel restaurant on Saturday at eight in the evening."

"Will do," I said. "See you then."

"Okay. Bye." She hung up the line and I returned the phone to its cradle.

"Who was that?" my mom asked.

"A girl," I said.

She gave me a look.

I sighed. "Her name is Katie. She's Hannah's cousin. She went with us to Texas."

"Hm," my mom said. "Sounds like you have a date."

I blushed. "Yeah," I said. "Sounds like it."

As I PACKED my bag for the weekend trip to Indianapolis, my brother knocked on my door. "Hey," he said. "Got your oil changed. Ready for the road."

"Thank you," I said.

"That Lando guy? He did a good job on that alternator."

After I got back from Agloe, we talked a lot about Dad and the things we missed about him. Our relationship was different now too, and, for the first time, it felt like we had a mutual respect for each other.

"That's good to hear," I said. "He seemed like a good guy."

"I hope you guys sell a ton of comic books," he said. "Maybe finally upgrade the sound system in that shitbox."

I laughed. "There's nothing wrong with my sound system *or* my car."

"Also, I found something," he said.

In his hand, he held out a photograph. I took it and felt myself choke up. It was the four of us from when Jake and

I were little—six and four years old respectively—and we were sitting at a picnic table. There was a birthday cake in front of Jake, who was in the middle of blowing the half-dozen candles.

"I remember this," I said. "You got that Transformer and I was sad because I wanted it."

"We played with that thing for hours that day," he said. "I knew then that I wanted to work on cars. Seeing all the parts on that thing made me want to find out everything I could about them."

"And it made me want to design my own characters," I said. "Even then, I drew boxes that were supposed to be cars that turned into robots. I made up my own stories about them and everything. Where did you find this?"

"In the bottom of my toolbox," he said. Then, with a sigh, "I miss him all the time."

"I do too," I said. "Every day."

"He'd be really proud of you, you know," he said. "I know that we haven't always got along, but I know Dad would be really proud. He always hung your drawings on the fridge."

"Not just me," I said. "Look at you. How much you've taken care of mom over the last few years. And you know he'd be out there with you now, working on a project, wiring up some speaker system that would blow the neighborhood away."

Jake laughed. "He did like loud music."

"Yeah he did." I looked at my watch. "Alright, I've got to hit the road."

"Good luck," he said. He held out a fist and I tapped it with my own.

As I stepped out the door, he called out to me. "Actually, what is it you nerds say? May the Force be with you?"

"You know," I said, "you keep that up and we might eventually let you into our club."

CHAPTER 32

I WAS EXHAUSTED. AFTER RUNNING THE CHEWIE'S Comics booth all day with Dustin, Joel and Hannah, I couldn't wait to return to my hotel room and crash on the bed with a comic book. We sold more of our inventory than we had anticipated, collectors swarming our booth and thumbing through the boxes, buying them by the handful. Every single customer was also given a flyer for the website, so we hoped that it would draw more traffic and sales.

So though I was looking forward to resting, I was looking forward to this even more. I hadn't seen Katie in over a month and though I had thought about her every day since we returned from Agloe, I didn't know if she felt the same.

Then, I saw her. She entered the restaurant, looked around and saw me sitting in the booth by myself. Her face lit up, answering my unspoken questions immediately. I waved at her and she came over to me.

She was dressed in a simple black dress, and her hair was let down, falling over her shoulders. The pink strip in it was gone. She had a bright eyeliner on and was a sharp contrast to the dark colors of her attire.

Behind her, a man followed close behind. Probably in his mid-thirties, he wore a suit jacket over a Thundercats t-shirt, his hair styled in a faux-hawk, the same almond-shaped eyes that she had.

I stood up to greet them.

"Hey," Katie said as she came to the table. Then, she held out her arms and we hugged, at first awkward, but settled into a familiar feeling.

"Hi," I said. "It's been a little while. How are you?"

"I'm good," she said. "And yes, it has been a while."

She stepped back and gestured to the man behind her. "This," she said, "is my uncle. Bryan, this is Josh."

He held out his hand and I shook it. He was immediately friendly, with one of those smiles that was warm and charming.

"Nice to meet you, Josh," he said. "I'm Bryan Chen. I've heard a lot of great things about you."

"Uh," I started. "Thank you." Then I gestured to the booth. "Would you guys like to have a seat? They haven't taken my order yet."

"Thank you," Bryan said. He slid into the seat across from mine and took up the menu, flipping through its pages.

I sat as well and Katie took the spot next to me. Having

her this close to me brought back memories of our roadtrip, of being in the ocean together.

"Have you seen the Chewie's booth yet?" I asked Katie, taking a sip from my water glass.

"Not yet," she said. "We've been at the Dark Horse booth all day."

"Dark Horse?" I said, confused. "You're here with Dark Horse?"

Dark Horse Comics was one of the most popular independent comic publishers. Their biggest title was *Star Wars*, which they'd taken over from Marvel in the early 90's.

"Bryan works for Dark Horse," Katie said.

I felt my eyebrows raise in surprise. "Wow," I said. "You never told me that." I turned to him. "I had no idea."

Working for a comic publisher, much less one like Dark Horse, that put out some of my favorite series, would be a dream come true.

"That's actually why we've asked you to meet us," Bryan said.

The waiter came to the table and, dropping off water for Katie and Bryan, took our orders. It gave me a moment to process what was going on. I wasn't just seeing my friend—I was sitting with someone from one of the major comic publishers.

Bryan, after taking a drink from his water glass, continued, "Katie showed me the book you were working on."

I gave her a look, knowing that my eyes were as wide as the saucers on the table.

"Don't worry," Bryan said. "Here's the thing, I'll get right to the chase. It's good. It's really good. I personally think it's incredibly imaginative while still staying true to the tropes of space opera. The whole 'holy grail in space' thing? Genius. We think your story, given a little professional polish, would do well as part of Dark Horse's catalogue."

"You..." I started, trying to wrap my mind around what he was saying. "You want my book? Like to publish?"

"That's exactly right," he said.

"Bryan is the acquisitions editor for the company," Katie said. "Remember when I asked if I could keep your book? I took it because I wanted to show him. I knew he would like it."

"And I do," he said. "Josh, I am prepared to offer you a publishing contract with Dark Horse Comics for your book plus two more future titles."

My mind went blank, my hands numb. There was no way this was happening.

"The contract comes with a hefty advance. From what Katie tells me, you are wishing to attend the art institute in Indianapolis this fall?"

"I was," I said, "but I couldn't pay for tuition. So I'm going to save money for a year and try to go next fall."

"You will be able to study with some of the best visual artists in the country, and we don't want you to have to wait just because of finances. That is why, along with the advance, Dark Horse will be completely subsidizing your tuition."

"What?" I said. It was more a statement of disbelief than a question. I felt my chin tremble, my heart swelling in my chest. "You can't be serious."

"One hundred percent serious, Josh," Bryan said. "We are committed to investing in you and your art because we think you have that *it* factor. We don't want to see you get swooped up by some other studio or publisher who won't see your talent for what it is, or who wouldn't invest in that talent the way Dark Horse will. We also would like for you to work with and apprentice under our *Star Wars* story group. I think you'd make a great addition to their team."

I felt like I was going to pass out. This rush of blood went to my head and I had to blink a few times to make sure I was still conscious. "I," started, "have to talk with my mom."

"Of course. We don't even have the contract written. But I wanted to meet you in person," Bryan said. "Katie talks very highly of you."

"Wait a minute," I said. "If you're her uncle," I turned to Katie, "and Hannah is your cousin..."

Katie laughed. "No, Hannah is on the Nguyen side. Bryan in on the Chen side. Our moms are sisters."

Beneath the table, she took my hand in hers and gave it a squeeze. "I have to be honest though. Hannah would always talk about this comic book artist friend of hers, and I always just kind of blew it off. But, no, you're the real deal."

I blushed again.

"I do have one request," I said.

"Name it."

"If I sign this contract, I want it put in that Chewie's Comics gets the exclusive first-run distribution for variant covers for any of my books."

"That's it?" Bryan asked.

"Uh," I said, confused. "Yeah. I think so. Why, is that not possible?"

Bryan laughed. "No, I think that's very doable. Most guys ask for a Miata or something."

I turned red but Katie nudged me. "Are you sure? Nothing that won't break down between here and Texas?" she said playfully.

"No, I'm pretty happy with the car I have. Lots of memories in that thing."

"I bet that's something we can do," Bryan said. "We always are looking for distribution partners that will help with the buzz of a new release in a unique way."

The waiter brought our orders—steak and potatoes for me, lobster for both Bryan and Katie—and we started eating. The conversation went from business to the roadtrip.

"Can I ask you something?" Bryan said.

"Of course."

He leaned in, speaking in almost a whisper. "Did you guys really hold it in your hands? The Boba Fett?"

"We did," I said, nodding, stabbing at my potatoes.

"Wow," he said. "What was it like?"

"It was like winning the lottery," I said. "But with someone else's ticket."

He leaned back in the booth. "Do you know how many guys have dreamed about owning that action figure?"

"I have a pretty good idea."

"And you guys just...gave it back. Incredible. I couldn't have done it. I mean, I would like to think that in that moment, I would do the right thing. But I don't know."

As we ate, the conversation turned to Dark Horse, the comic book and eventually about the industry as a whole. He was excited about an online comic book retailer and what it would do for distribution.

"Someday, you'll probably see comic books delivered completely digitally," he said. "And you'll read them on your computer."

I couldn't imagine that. I loved holding the pictures in my hands, turning the pages, going to the comic book shop to pick up my weekly orders. Still, it made sense. Already, most music was available on the internet and Apple had released some kind of mp3 player that you could carry in your pocket that could hold a thousand songs. The digital revolution would come swiftly for comic books as well, he said, and Dark Horse was ready to be on the front end of it.

After the waiter brought the check, Bryan paid for all of our meals. He told me that a draft of the contract would be mailed to me before the end of the week and that we could spend as much time as we needed to look it over.

This won't come as a surprise, but I didn't need much time at all.

After dinner, Katie walked with me to my hotel room. I felt like I was striding on air, my feet barely touching the ground. The whole way up the elevator and down the hall to the room I shared with Joel and Dustin, I almost skipped. As we walked, Katie's hand found mine, our fingers interlacing.

When we reached the door to the room, she knocked.

"You don't have to knock," I said. As I reached into my pocket to get my key, the door swung open. Joel, Dustin and Hannah were in there. A banner hung across the entry and there was confetti everywhere.

"Congratulations!" they all shouted in unison, pulling me in with a group hug.

"Thanks, guys." Then, I pulled back. "Wait a minute," I said. "You all were in on this? You knew that Katie had her uncle and..." I trailed off.

"Dude," Dustin said, "you won't believe how many times I almost spilled the beans."

"Yeah, he's the worst secret-keeper," Hannah said. "But yes, we knew. And we definitely are going to put your book front and center on the website!"

I turned to Katie. "So I guess this means you really liked that comic?"

"Of course I did," she said. "When I finished it, I knew I needed to give it to Uncle Bryan."

"I remember you telling me your uncle got you into comic books, but I guess I never put it together that he was actually in the industry," I said.

"I tried not to say too much about him or about what he does for a living. I didn't want to feel like you just wanted to be my friend because of him. I have had too many guys try to get close with me because they knew that he had the newest comic books before anyone else, or he could somehow get them in the industry," she said.

"I get that," I said.

"But hey, you know what this means, don't you?" Katie said, nudging me with her shoulder. "We'll both in Indianapolis this fall."

"Which means we'll get to do a lot more of this." I pulled her in for a kiss. It was this immediate thing, overwhelmed with the excitement of the comic book shop, getting my tuition paid for, and seeing her again. All of it rushed to my head.

Our lips met and then she pulled back, looking at me like I had done something crazy. But then, she smiled and kissed me again.

I heard my friends gasp and then whoop in excitement.

And let me tell you, I'd trade every action figure in the world for that.

THE END

BOOK CLUB GUIDE

TO THE KING OF ACTION FIGURES

1. Josh and his brother Jake have a seemingly contentious relationship early in the book. How does Josh's acceptance of what happened to his family change that perception later in the story?

2. Josh talks about the "miracle" of Star Wars. Why do you think he considers it a miracle?

3. Josh is apprehensive to join his friends on the roadtrip. How does his risk-aversion affect his relationship with them? And where did that risk-aversion stem from?

4. Which character in the book do you identify with the most?

5. Have you ever taken a roadtrip with friends? What were some of the events that went awry? How did you respond to that?

6. Josh comes to terms with the death of his father and how it affected his life. How did Jan's estate sale bring him to that state of mind?

7. Have you ever found a rare item at an estate sale? What would you do if you did?

ACKNOWLEDGMENTS

I discovered *Star Wars* when I was nine years old and it changed my life. Growing up in the public library, I was so excited to find out that there were novels that took place after the movies. I devoured them. I wanted to write my own. I still might someday. To the fine folks at Disney—I await your call.

Many of the places referenced in this novel are real, but Agloe, TX is not. It is based on Agloe, NY, a "paper town" that was made famous in John Green's novel *Paper Towns*. That book is one of my favorite road-trip stories ever written and this is my attempt at homage to him.

I have a lot of people to thank in this section, but first and foremost, I want to thank my sweet wife Jennifer, who has stood by me when I have been at my lowest, who has always been supportive and loving through everything. She was the person to push me toward writing my first novel back in 2018.

Thank you to all the independent bookstores who have been supportive over the last few years. Burrowing Owl in

Amarillo, TX; The Book Burrow in Pflugerville, TX; Sundog Book in Seaside, FL; Ferguson Books in Fargo, ND—all of you have been incredible and kind and I can't thank you enough for stocking my books and sharing them with readers.

In no particular order, thank you:

Gabe Morgan
Jerry McKee
Gordon Clark
Lindsey Jesionowski
Alisha Emrich
Allison Spooner
Russell Camp
Sterling Miller
Dane Ferguson
Dallas Bell
James Brown
Danny Scott
The Smoke Easy Guys

Apologies to Derek Porterfield, there simply wasn't enough room in these pages to thank you.

ABOUT THE AUTHOR

Andrew J Brandt is the Pencraft award-winning and bestselling author of multiple novels, including the Reading the West award nominees *Palo Duro* and *Mixtape for the End of the World*. His 2022 release *Picture Unavailable* spent four weeks as Amazon's #1 new YA release and received a Book-Fest Award in the YA Category upon publication. He is an on-air contributor for KAMR-NBC4's *Studio 4* program in Amarillo, TX where he hosts a monthly book club segment. His novels have been optioned for television and film. A graduate of West Texas A&M University, Andrew resides in Texas with his wife and children.

Find Andrew online at www.andrewjbrandt.com

ALSO BY ANDREW J BRANDT

YOUNG ADULT

The Treehouse

The Abduction of Sarah Phillips

Palo Duro

Mixtape for the End of the World

Picture Unavailable

FOR ADULTS

In the Fog

The Unwinding Cable Car

AS ELLIOTT ANDREWS

All the Right Notes

www.ingramcontent.com/pod-product-compliance
Lightning Source LLC
Chambersburg PA
CBHW020558310726
48979CB00008B/1264/J

* 9 7 8 1 7 3 7 3 4 8 7 5 7 *